The

Provincial Lady

in Wartime

Robert still dissatisfied. Tells me Cook's nose is in quite the wrong place.

The PROVINCIAL LADY *in* Wartime

by

E. M. DELAFIELD

ILLUSTRATED BY
LESLIE GILBERT ILLINGWORTH

Cassandra Editions

Published in 1986 by
Academy Chicago Publishers
425 North Michigan Avenue
Chicago, Illinois 60611

Library of Congress Cataloging-in-Publication Data

Delafield, E. M., 1890-1943.
    The provincial lady in wartime.

    1. World War, 1939-1945—Fiction.   I. Title.
PR6007.E33P74   1986   823'.912   86-22140
ISBN 0-89733-210-5 (pbk.)

ILLUSTRATIONS

[vii]

Illustrations

The
Provincial Lady
in WARTIME

The
Provincial Lady
in WARTIME

September 1st, 1939.—Enquire of Robert
whether he does not think that, in view of times
in which we live, diary of daily events might
not be of ultimate historical value to posterity.
He replies that It Depends.

Explain that I do not mean events of national importance, which may safely be left
to the Press, but only chronicle of ordinary English citizen's reactions to war which now appears
inevitable.

Robert's only reply—if reply it can be called
—is to enquire whether I am really quite certain that Cook takes a medium size in gas-
masks. Personally, he should have thought a
large, if not out-size, was indicated. Am forced
to realise that Cook's gas-mask is intrinsically
of greater importance than problematical contribution to literature by myself, but am all

the same slightly aggrieved. Better nature fortunately prevails, and I suggest that Cook had better be asked to clear up the point once and for all. Inclination on the part of Robert to ring the bell has to be checked, and I go instead to kitchen passage door and ask if Cook will please come here for a moment.

She does come, and Robert selects frightful-looking appliances, each with a snout projecting below a little talc window, from pile which has stood in corner of the study for some days.

Cook shows a slight inclination towards coyness when Robert adjusts one on her head with stout crosspiece, and replies from within, when questioned, that It'll do nicely, sir, thank you. (Voice sounds very hollow and sepulchral.)

Robert still dissatisfied and tells me that Cook's nose is in quite the wrong place, and he always thought it would be, and that what she needs is a large size. Cook is accordingly extracted from the medium-size, and emerges looking heated, and much inclined to say that she'd rather make do with this one if it's all the same to us, and get back to her fish-cakes before they're spoilt. This total misapprehension as to the importance of the situation is rather sharply dealt with by Robert, as A.R.P.[1] Organiser for the district, and he again inducts Cook into a gas-mask and this time declares the results to be much more satisfactory.

Cook (evidently thinks Robert most unreasonable) asserts that she's sure it'll do beautifully—this surely very curious adverb to select? —and departs with a look implying that she has been caused to waste a good deal of valuable time.

Cook's gas-mask is put into cardboard box and marked with her name, and a similar provision made for everybody in the house, after which Robert remarks, rather strangely, that *that's* a good job done.

Telephone bell rings, Vicky can be heard rushing to answer it, and shortly afterwards appears, looking delighted, to say that that was Mr. Humphrey Holloway, the billeting-officer, to say that we may expect three evacuated children and one teacher from East Poplar at eleven o'clock to-night.

Have been expecting this, in a way, for days

[1] Air Raid Precaution.

[3]

and days, and am fully prepared to take it with
absolute calm, and am therefore not pleased
when Vicky adopts an *air capable* and says:
It'll be all right, I'm not to throw a fit, she can
easily get everything ready. (Dear Vicky in
many ways a great comfort, and her position as
House prefect at school much to her credit, but
cannot agree to be treated as though already in
advanced stage of senile decay.)

I answer repressively that she can help me
to get the beds made up, and we proceed to top-
floor attics, hitherto occupied by Robin, who
has now, says Vicky, himself been evacuated
to erstwhile spare bedroom.

Make up four beds, already erected by Robin
and the gardener in corners, as though about to
play Puss-in-the-Corner, and collect as many
mats from different parts of the house as can
be spared, and at least two that can't. Vicky
undertakes to put flowers in each room before
nightfall, and informs me that picture of Infant Samuel on the wall is *definitely* old-fashioned and must go. Feel sentimental about this
and inclined to be slightly hurt, until she suddenly rather touchingly adds that, as a matter
of fact, she thinks she would like to have it in

her own room—to which we accordingly re-move it.

Robin returns from mysterious errand to the village, for which he has borrowed the car, looks all round the rooms rather vaguely and says: Everything seems splendid—which I think is over-estimating the amenities provided, which consist mainly of very old nursery screen with pictures pasted on it, green rush-bottomed chairs, patchwork quilts and painted white furniture. He removes his trouser-press with an air of deep concern and announces, as he goes, that the evacuated children can read all his books if they want to. Look round at volumes of Aldous Huxley, André Maurois, Neo-Georgian Poets, the *New Yorker* and a number of Greek text-books, and remove them all.

Inspection of the schoolroom—also to be devoted to evacuated children—follows, and I am informed by Vicky that they may use the rocking-horse, the doll's house, and all the toys, but that she has locked the book-cases. Am quite unable to decide whether I should, or should not, attempt interference here.

(Remembrance awakens, quite involuntarily,

of out-moded educational methods adopted by Mr. Fairchild. But results, on the whole, not what one would wish to see, and dismiss the recollection at once.)

Vicky asks whether she hadn't better tell Cook, Winnie and May about the arrival of what she calls "The little evacuments," and I say Certainly, and am extremely relieved at not having to do it myself. Call after her that she is to say they will want a hot meal on arrival but that if Cook will leave the things out, I will get it ready myself and nobody is to sit up.

Reply reaches me later to the effect that Cook will be sitting up in *any* case, to listen-in to any announcements that may be made on the wireless.

Announcement, actually, is made at six o'clock of general mobilisation in England and France.

I say, Well, it's a relief it's come at last, Robin delivers a short speech about the Balkan States and their political significance, which is not, he thinks, sufficiently appreciated by the Government—and Vicky declares that if there's a war, she ought to become a **V.A.D.** and not go back to school.

Robert says nothing.

Very shortly afterwards he becomes extremely active over the necessity of conforming to the black-out regulations, and tells me that from henceforward no chink of light must be allowed to show from any window whatever.

He then instructs us all to turn on every light in the house and draw all the blinds and curtains while he makes a tour of inspection outside. We all obey in frenzied haste, as though a fleet of enemy aircraft had already been sighted making straight for this house and no other, and then have to wait some fifteen minutes before Robert comes in again and says that practically every curtain in the place will have to be lined with black and that sheets of brown paper must be nailed up over several of the windows. Undertake to do all before nightfall to-morrow, and make a note to get in supply of candles, matches, and at least two electric torches.

Telephone rings again after dinner, and con-

[1] Voluntary Aid Detachment.

viction overwhelms me that I am to receive information of world-shaking importance, probably under oath of secrecy. Call turns out to be, once more, from Mr. Holloway, to say that evacuees are not expected before midnight. Return to paper-games with Robin and Vicky.

Telephone immediately rings again.

Aunt Blanche, speaking from London, wishes to know if we should care to take her as paying guest for the duration of the war. It isn't, she says frenziedly, that she would *mind* being bombed, or is in the least afraid of anything that Hitler—who is, she feels perfectly certain, simply the Devil in disguise—may do to her, but the friend with whom she shares a flat has joined up as an Ambulance driver and says that she will be doing twenty-four-hour shifts, and sleeping on a camp bed in the Adelphia, and that as the lease of their flat will be up on September 25th, they had better give it up. The friend, to Aunt Blanche's certain knowledge, will never see sixty-five again, and Aunt Blanche has protested strongly against the whole scheme —but to no avail. Pussy—Mrs. Winter-Gammon—has bought a pair of slacks and been given an armlet, and may be called up at any moment.

I express whole-hearted condemnation of Mrs. Winter-Gammon—whom I have never liked—and put my hand over the mouthpiece of the telephone to hiss at Robert that it's Aunt Blanche, and she wants to come as P.G., and Robert looks rather gloomy but finally nods— like Jove—and I tell Aunt Blanche how delighted we shall all be to have her here as long as she likes.

Aunt Blanche thanks us all—sounding tear-ful—and repeats again that it isn't *air-raids* she minds—not for one minute—and enquires if Robin is nineteen yet—which he won't be for nearly a year. She then gives me quantities of information about relations and acquaintances.

William is an A.R.P.[1] Warden and Angela is acting as his skeleton staff—which Aunt Blanche thinks has a very odd sound. Emma Hay is said to be looking for a job as Organiser, but what she wants to organise is not known. Old Uncle A. has refused to leave London and has offered his services to the War Office, but in

[1] Air Raid Precautions.

[9]

view of his age—eighty-two—is afraid that he may not be sent on active service.

She asks what is happening to Caroline Concannon, that nice Rose and Poor Cissie Crabbe.

Rose is still in London, I tell her, and will no doubt instantly find Hospital work—Caroline married years ago and went to Kenya and is tiresome about never answering letters—and Cissie Crabbe I haven't seen or heard of for ages.

Very likely not, replies Aunt Blanche in a lugubrious voice, but at a time like this one is bound to recollect old ties. Can only return a respectful assent to this, but do not really see the force of it.

Aunt Blanche then tells me about old Mrs. Winter-Gammon all over again, and I make much the same comments as before, and she further reverts to her attitude about air-raids. Perceive that this conversation is likely to go on all night unless steps are taken to check Aunt Blanche decisively, and I therefore tell her that we are expecting a party of evacuees at any moment—(can distinctly hear Vicky exclaiming loudly: Not till midnight—exclamation no doubt equally audible to Aunt Blanche)—and that I *must* ring off.

Of course, of course, cries Aunt Blanche, but she just felt she *had* to have news of all of us, because at a time like this ——

Can see nothing for it but to replace receiver sharply, hoping she may think we have been cut off by exchange.

Return to paper-games and am in the midst of searching my mind for famous Admiral whose name begins with D—nothing but Nelson occurs to me—when I perceive that Robin is smoking a pipe.

Am most anxious to let dear Robin develop along his own lines without undue interference, but am inwardly shattered by this unexpected sight, and by rather green tinge all over his face. Do not say anything, but all hope of discovering Admiral whose name begins with D has now left me, as mind definitely—though temporarily, I hope—refuses to function.

Shortly afterwards pipe goes out, but Robin —greener than ever—relights it firmly. Vicky says Isn't it marvellous, he got it in the village this afternoon—at which Robin looks at me with rather apologetic smile, and I feel the least I can do is to smile back again. Am rather better after this.

Vicky embarks on prolonged discussion as to desirability or otherwise of her sitting up till twelve to receive little evacuments, when front-door bell peals violently, and everyone except Robert says: Here they are!

Winnie can be heard flying along kitchen passage at quite unprecedented speed, never before noticeable when answering any bell whatever, and almost instantly appears to say that Robert is Wanted, please—which sounds like a warrant for his arrest, or something equally dramatic.

Vicky at once says that it's quite impossible for her to go to bed till she knows what it is.

Robin re-lights pipe, which has gone out for the seventh time.

Suspense is shortly afterwards relieved when Robert reappears in drawing-room and says that a crack of light is distinctly visible through the pantry window and a special constable has called to say that it must immediately be extinguished.

[12]

Vicky asks in awed tones how he knew about it and is told briefly that he was making his rounds, and we are all a good deal impressed by so much promptitude and efficiency. Later on, Robert tells me privately that special constable was only young Leslie Oakford from the Home Farm, and that he has been told not to make so much noise another time. Can see that Robert is in slight state of conflict between patriotic desire to obey all regulations, and private inner conviction that young Leslie is making a nuisance of himself. Am glad to note that patriotism prevails, and pantry light is replaced by sinister-looking blue bulb and heavily draped shade.

Telephone rings once more—Humphrey Holloway thinks, apologetically, that we may like to know that evacuated children now not expected at all, but may be replaced next Monday by three young babies and one mother. Can only say Very well, and ask what has happened. Humphrey Holloway doesn't know. He adds that all is very difficult, and one hundred and forty children evacuated to Bude are said to have arrived at very small, remote moorland village instead. One the other hand, Miss Pankerton—who asked for six boys—has got them, and is reported to be very happy. (Can only hope the six boys are, too.) Lady B.—whose house could very well take in three dozen—has announced that she is turning it into a Convalescent Home for Officers, and can therefore receive no evacuees at all. Am indignant at this, and say so, but H. H. evidently too weary for anything but complete resignation, and simply replies that many of the teachers are more difficult than the children, and that the mothers are the worst of all.

(Mental note here, to the effect that no more unpopular section of the community exists, anywhere, than mothers as a whole.)

Robert, when told that evacuees are *not* coming to-night, says Thank God and we prepare to go upstairs when Vicky makes dramatic appearance in vest and pants and announces that there is No Blind in the W.C. Robert points out, shortly and sharply, that no necessity exists for turning on the light at all, Vicky disagrees and is disposed to argue the point, and I beg her to retire to bed instantly.

Impression prevails as of having lived

through at least two European wars since morning, but this view certainly exaggerated and will doubtless disperse after sleep.

September 3rd, 1939.—England at war with Germany. Announcement is made by Prime Minister over the radio at eleven-fifteen and is heard by us in village church, where wireless has been placed on the pulpit.

Everyone takes it very quietly and general feeling summed up by old Mrs. S. at the Post Office who says to me, after mentioning that her two sons have both been called up: Well, we've got to *show* 'Itler, haven't we? Agree, emphatically, that we have.

September 7th.—Discuss entire situation as it affects ourselves with Robert, the children and Cook.

Robert says: Better shut up the house as we shan't be able to afford to live anywhere, after the war—but is brought round to less drastic views and agrees to shutting up drawing-room and two bedrooms only. He also advocates letting one maid go—which is as well since both have instantly informed me that they feel it their duty to leave and look for war work.

[15]

Cook displays unexpectedly sporting spirit, pats me on the shoulder with quite unprecedented familiarity, and assures me that I'm not to worry—she'll see me through, whatever happens. Am extremely touched and inclined to shed tears. Will Cook agree to let Aunt Blanche take over the housekeeping, if Robert is away all day, the children at school, and I am doing war work in London and coming down here one week out of four? (This course indicated by absolute necessity of earning some money if possible, and inability to remain out of touch with current happenings in London.)

Yes, Cook declares stoutly, she will agree to anything and she quite understands how I'm situated. (Hope that some time or other she may make this equally clear to me.) We evolve hurried scheme for establishment of Aunt Blanche, from whom nothing as to date of arrival has as yet been heard, and for weekly Help for the Rough from the village.

Cook also asserts that May can do as she likes, but Winnie is a silly girl who doesn't know what's good for her, and she thinks she can talk her round all right. She *does* talk her

[16]

round, and Winnie announces a change of mind and says she'll be glad to stay on, please. Should much like to know how Cook accomplished this, but can probably never hope to do so.

Spend most of the day listening to News from the wireless and shutting up the drawing-room and two bedrooms, which involves moving most of the smaller furniture into the middle of the room and draping everything with dust-sheets.

Robin—still dealing with pipe, which goes out oftener than ever—has much to say about enlisting, and Vicky, equally urgent—with less foundation—on undesirability of her returning to school. School, however, telegraphs to say that reopening will take place as usual, on appointed date.

September 8th.—Am awakened at 1.10 A.M. by telephone. Imagination, as usual, runs riot and while springing out of bed, into dressing-gown and downstairs, has had ample time to present air-raid, assembly of household in the cellar, incendiary bombs, house in flames and all buried beneath the ruins. Collide with Robert on the landing—he says briefly that It's probably an

A.R.P.[1] call and dashes down, and I hear him snatch up receiver.

Reach the telephone myself in time to hear him say Yes he'll come at once. He'll get out the car. He'll be at the station in twenty minutes' time.

What station?

Robert hangs up the receiver and informs me that that was the station-master. An old lady has arrived from London, the train having taken twelve hours to do the journey—usually accomplished in five—and says that we are expecting her, she sent a telegram. She is, the station-master thinks, a bit upset.

I ask in a dazed way if it's an evacuee, and Robert says No, it's Aunt Blanche, and the telegram must, like the train, have been delayed.

Am torn between compassion for Aunt Blanche—station-master's description almost certainly an understatement—and undoubted dismay at unpropitious hour of her arrival. Can see nothing for it but to assure Robert—untruthfully—that I can Easily Manage, and will have everything ready by the time he's back

[1] Air Raid Precautions.

[18]

Aunt Blanche arrives.

from station. This is accomplished without awakening household, and make mental note to the effect that air-raid warning itself will probably leave Cook and Winnie quite impervious and serenely wrapped in slumber.

Proceed to make up bed in North Room, recently swathed by my own hands in dust-sheets and now rapidly disinterred, put in hot-water bottle, and make tea and cut bread-and-butter. (*N.B.:* State of kitchen, as to cleanliness and tidiness, gratifying. Larder less good, and why four half-loaves of stale bread standing uncovered on shelf? Also note that cat, Thompson, evidently goes to bed nightly on scullery shelf. Hope that Robert, who to my certain knowledge puts Thompson out every night, will never discover this.)

Have agreeable sense of having dealt promptly and efficiently with war emergency—this leads to speculation as to which Ministerial Department will put me in charge of its workings, and idle vision of taking office as Cabinet Minister and Robert's astonishment at appointment. Memory, for no known reason, at this point recalls the fact that Aunt Blanche will

want hot water to wash in and that I have forgotten to provide any. Hasten to repair omission
—boiler fire, as I expected, practically extinct
and I stoke it up and put on another kettle and
fetch can from bathroom. (Brass cans all in need
of polish, and enamel ones all chipped. Am discouraged.)

Long wait ensues, and drink tea prepared for
Aunt Blanche myself, and put on yet another
kettle. Decide that I shall have time to dress, go
upstairs, and immediately hear car approaching
and dash down again. Car fails to materialise
and make second excursion, which results in unpleasant discovery in front of the mirror that
my hair is on end and my face pale blue with
cold. Do the best I can to repair ravages of the
night, though not to much avail, and put on
clothes.

On reaching dining-room, find that electric
kettle has boiled over and has flooded the carpet. Abandon all idea of Ministerial appointment and devote myself to swabbing up hot
water, in the midst of which car returns. Opening of front door reveals that both headlights
have turned blue and emit minute ray of pallid

light only. This effect achieved by Robert unknown to me, and am much impressed.

Aunt Blanche is in tears, and has brought three suitcases, one bundle of rugs, a small wooden box, a portable typewriter, a hat-box and a trunk. She is in deep distress and says that she would have spent the night in the station willingly, but the station-master wouldn't let her. Station-master equally adamant at her suggestion of walking to the Hotel—other end of the town—and assured her it was full of the Militia. Further offer from Aunt Blanche of walking about the streets till breakfast-time also repudiated and telephone call accomplished by strong-minded station-master without further attention to her protests.

I tell Aunt Blanche five separate times how glad I am to have her, and that we are not in the least disturbed by nocturnal arrival, and finally lead her into the dining-room where she is restored by tea and bread-and-butter. Journey, she asserts, was terrible—train crowded, but everyone good-tempered—no food, but what can you expect in war-time?—and she hopes I won't think she has brought too much luggage.

[21]

No, not at all—because she *has* two *large* trunks, but they are waiting at the station.

Take Aunt Blanche to the North Room, on entering which she again cries a good deal but says it is only because I am so kind and I mustn't think her in any way unnerved because that's the last thing she ever is—and get to bed at 3.15.

Hot-water bottle cold as a stone and cannot imagine why I didn't refill it, but not worth going down again. Later on decide that it *is* worth going down again, but don't do so. Remainder of the night passed in similar vacillations.

September 12th.—Aunt Blanche settling down, and national calamity evidently bringing out best in many of us, Cook included, but exception must be made in regard to Lady Boxe, who keeps large ambulance permanently stationed in drive and says that house is to be a Hospital (Officers only) and is therefore not available for evacuees. No officers materialise, but Lady B. reported to have been seen in full Red Cross uniform with snow-white veil floating in the breeze behind her. (Undoubtedly very trying colour next to any but a youthful face; but am not proud of this reflection and keep it to myself.)

Everybody else in neighbourhood has received evacuees, most of whom arrive without a word of warning and prove to be of age and sex diametrically opposite to those expected.

Rectory turns its dining-room into a dormitory and Our Vicar's Wife struggles gallantly with two mothers and three children under five, one of whom is thought to be suffering from fits. Both her maids have declared that they must find war work and immediately departed in search of it. I send Vicky up to see what she can do, and she is proved to be helpful, practical, and able to keep a firm hand over the under-fives.

Am full of admiration for Our Vicar's Wife and very sorry for her, but feel she is at least better off than Lady Frobisher, who rings up to ask me if I know how one gets rid of *lice*? Refer her to the chemist, who tells me later that if he has been asked that question once in the last week, he's been asked it twenty times.

Elderly neighbours, Major and Mrs. Bergery,

recent arrivals at small house in the village, are given two evacuated teachers and appear in consequence to be deeply depressed. The teachers sit about and drink cups of tea and assert that the organisation at the *London* end was wonderful, but at *this* end there isn't any organisation at all. Moreover, they are here to teach—which they do for about four hours in the day—but not for anything else. Mrs. Bergery suggests that they should collect all the evacuated children in the village and play with them, but this not well received.

Our Vicar, appealed to by the Major, calls on the teachers and effects a slight improvement. They offer, although without much enthusiasm, to organise an hour of Recreative Education five days a week. He supposes, says Our Vicar, that this means play, and closes with the suggestion at once.

Light relief is afforded by Miss Pankerton, who is, we all agree, having the time of her life. Miss P.—who has, for no known reason, sprung into long blue trousers and leather jerkin —strides about the village marshalling six pallid and wizened little boys from Bethnal Green in front of her. Extraordinary legend is current that she has taught them to sing "Under a spreading chestnut-tree, the village smithy stands," and that they roar it in chorus with great docility in her presence, but have a version of their own which she has accidentally over-heard from the bathroom and that this runs:

> Under a spreading chestnut-tree
> Stands the bloody A.R.P.[1]
> So says the ——ing B.B.C.[2]

Aunt Blanche, in telling me this, adds that: "It's really wonderful, considering the eldest is only seven years old." Surely a comment of rather singular leniency?

Our own evacuees make extraordinarily brief appearance, coming—as usual—on day and at hour when least expected, and consisting of menacing-looking woman with twins of three and baby said to be eighteen months old but looking more like ten weeks. Mother comes into the open from the very beginning, saying that she doesn't fancy the country, and it will upset the children, and none of it is what she's

[1] Air Raid Precautions.
[2] British Broadcasting Corporation.

accustomed to. Do my best for them with cups
of tea, cakes, toys for the children and flowers
in bedroom. Only the cups of tea afford even
moderate satisfaction, and mother leaves the
house at dawn next day to find Humphrey Holloway and inform him that he is to telegraph to
Dad to come and fetch them away immediately
—which he does twenty-four hours later. Feel
much cast-down, and apologise to H. H., who
informs me in reply that evacuees from all parts
of the country are hastening back to danger
zone as rapidly as possible, as being infinitely
preferable to rural hospitality. Where this *isn't*
happening, adds Humphrey in tones of deepest
gloom, it is the country hostesses who are proving inadequate and clamouring for the removal
of their guests.

Cannot believe this to be an accurate sum-
mary of the situation, and feel that Humphrey
is unduly pessimistic owing to overwork as
Billeting Officer. He admits this may be so,
and further says that, now he comes to think
of it, some of the families in village are quite
pleased with the London children. Adds—as
usual—that the *real* difficulty is the mothers.

They roar it in chorus with great docility in her presence.

Are we, I ask, to have other evacuees in place of departed failures? Try to sound as though I hope we are—but am only too well aware that effort is poor and could convince nobody. H. H. says that he will see what he can do, which I think equal, as a reply, to anything ever perpetrated by Roman oracle.

September 13th.—Question of evacuees solved by Aunt Blanche, who proposes that we should receive two children of Coventry clergyman and his wife, personally known to her, and their nurse. Children are charming, says Aunt Blanche —girls aged six and four—and nurse young Irish-woman about whom she knows nothing but that she is *not* a Romanist and is called Doreen Fitzgerald. Send cordial invitation to all three.

September 17th.—Installation of Doreen Fitzgerald, Marigold and Margery. Children pretty and apparently good. D. Fitzgerald has bright red hair but plain face and to all suggestions simply replies: Certainly I shall.

House and bedrooms once more reorganised, schoolroom temporarily reverts to being a nursery again—am inwardly delighted by this but

[27]

refrain from saying so—and D. Fitzgerald, asked if she will look after rooms herself, again repeats: Certainly I shall. Effect of this is one of slight patronage, combined with willing spirit.

Weather continues lovely, garden all Michaelmas daisies, dahlias and nasturtiums—autumn roses a failure, but cannot expect everything—and Aunt Blanche and I walk about under the apple-trees and round the tennis-court and ask one another who could ever believe that England is at war? Answer is, alas, only too evident—but neither of us makes it aloud.

Petrol rationing, which was to have started yesterday, postponed for a week. (*Query:* Is this an ingenious device for giving the whole country agreeable surprise, thereby improving public *morale*?) Robin and Vicky immediately point out that it is Vicky's last day at home, and ask if they couldn't go to a film and have tea at the café? Agree to this at once and am much moved by their delighted expressions of gratitude.

Long talk with Aunt Blanche occupies most of the afternoon. She has much to say about

[28]

Pussy—old Mrs. Winter-Gammon. Pussy, declares Aunt Blanche, has behaved neither wisely, considerately nor even with common decency. She may look many years younger than her age, but sixty-six is sixty-six and is *not* the proper time of life for driving a heavy ambulance. Pussy might easily be a grandmother. She *isn't* a grandmother, as it happens, because Providence has—wisely, thinks Aunt Blanche—withheld from her the blessing of children, but so far as age goes, she could very well be a grandmother ten times over.

Where, I enquire, are Mrs. Winter-Gammon and the ambulance in action?

Nowhere, cries Aunt Blanche. Mrs. W.-G. has pranced off in this irresponsible way to an A.R.P.[1] Station in the Adelphi—extraordinary place, all underground, somewhere underneath the Savoy—and so far has done nothing whatever except Stand By with crowds and crowds of others. She is on a twenty-four-hour shift and supposed to sleep on a camp-bed in a Women's Rest-room without any ventilation whatever in a pandemonium of noise. Suggest that if this

[1] Air Raid Precautions.

goes on long enough old Mrs. W.-G. will almost certainly become a nervous wreck before very long and be sent home incapacitated.

Aunt Blanche answers, rather curtly, that I don't know Pussy and that in any case the flat has now been given up and she herself has no intention of resuming life with Pussy. She has had more to put up with than people realise and it has now come to the parting of the ways. Opening here afforded leads me to discussion of plans with Aunt Blanche. Can she, and will she, remain on here in charge of household if I go to London and take up a job, preferably in the nature of speaking or writing, so that I can return home for, say, one week in every four? Cook—really pivot on whom the whole thing turns—has already expressed approval of the scheme.

Aunt Blanche—usually perhaps inclined to err on the side of indecisiveness—rises to the occasion magnificently and declares firmly that Of Course she will. She adds, in apt imitation of D. Fitzgerald, Certainly I shall—and we both laugh. Am startled beyond measure when she adds that it doesn't seem *right* that my abilities should be wasted down here, when they might be made use of in wider spheres by the Government. Can only hope that Government will take view similar to Aunt Blanche's.

Practical discussion follows, and I explain that dear Rose has asked me on a postcard, days ago, if I know anyone who might take over tiny two-roomed furnished flat in Buckingham Street, Strand, belonging to unknown cousin of her own, gone with R.N.V.R.[1] to East Africa. Have informed her, by telephone, that I might consider doing so myself, and will make definite pronouncement shortly.

Go! says Aunt Blanche dramatically. This is no time for making two bites at a cherry, and she herself will remain at the helm here and regard the welfare of Robert and the evacuated children as her form of national service. It seems to her more suited to the elderly, she adds rather caustically, than jumping into a pair of trousers and muddling about in an ambulance.

Think better to ignore this reference and content myself with thanking Aunt Blanche warmly. Suggest writing to Rose at once, se-

[1] Royal Naval Volunteer Reserve.

curing flat, but Aunt Blanche boldly advocates a trunk-call and says that this is a case of Vital Importance and in no way contrary to the spirit of national economy or Government's request to refrain from unnecessary telephoning.

Hours later, Aunt Blanche startles Marigold, Margery and myself—engaged in peacefully playing game of Happy Families—by emitting a scream and asking: Did I say *Buckingham* Street?

Yes, I did.

Then, I shall be positively next door to Adelphi, underworld, A.R.P.[1] Station, ambulance and Pussy. Within one minute's walk. But, what is far more important, I shall be able to see there delightful young friend, also standing by, to whom Aunt Blanche is devoted and of whom I must have heard her speak. Serena Thingamy.

Acknowledge Serena Thingamy—have never been told surname—but attention distracted by infant Margery who has remained glued to Happy Families throughout and now asks with brassy determination for Master Bones the Butcher's Son. Produce Master Potts by mis-

[1] Air Raid Precautions.

take, am rebuked gravely by Margery and screamed at by Marigold, and at the same time informed by Aunt Blanche that she can never remember the girl's name but I *must* know whom she means—dear little Serena Fiddle-dedee. Agree that I do, promise to go down into the underworld in search of her, and give full attention to collecting remaining unit of Mr. Bun the Baker's family.

Robin and Vicky come back after dark—I have several times visualised fearful car smash, and even gone so far as to compose inscription on tombstone—and declare that driving without any lights is absolutely *marvellous* and that film—*Beau Geste*—was super.

September 18th.—Departure of Vicky in the company of athletic-looking science mistress who meets her at Exeter station. Robin and I see them off, with customary sense of desolation, and console ourselves with cocoa and buns in the town. Robin then says he will meet me later, as he wishes to make enquiries about being placed on the Reserve of the Devon Regiment.

Am torn between pride, tenderness, incredulity and horror, but can only acquiesce.

September 20th.—Robin informed by military

authorities that he is to return to school for the present.

September 21st.—Am struck, not for the first time, by extraordinary way in which final arrangements never *are* final, but continue to lead on to still further activities until parallel with eternity suggests itself, and brain in danger of reeling.

Spend much time in consulting lists with which writing-desk is littered and trying to decipher mysterious abbreviations such as Sp. W. about T-cloths and Wind cl. in s. room, and give Aunt Blanche many directions as to care of evacuees and Robert's taste in breakfast dishes. No cereal on any account, and eggs not to be poached more than twice a week. Evacuees, on the other hand, require cereals every day and are said by Doreen Fitzgerald not to like bacon. Just as well, replies Aunt Blanche, as this is shortly to be rationed. This takes me into conversational byway concerning food shortage in Berlin, and our pity for the German people with whom, Aunt Blanche and I declare, we have no quarrel whatever, and who must on no account be identified with Nazi Party, let alone with Nazi Government. The whole thing, says Aunt Blanche, will be brought to an end by German revolution. I entirely agree, but ask when, to which she replies with a long story about Hitler's astrologer. Hitler's astrologer—a woman—has predicted every event in his career with astounding accuracy, and the Führer has consulted her regularly. Recently, however, she has—with some lack of discretion—informed him that his downfall, if not his assassination, is now a matter of months, and as a result, astrology has been forbidden in Germany. The astrologer is said to have disappeared.

Express suitable sentiments in return, and turn on wireless for the Four O'clock News. Am, I hope, duly appreciative of B.B.C.[1] Home Service, but struck by something a little unnatural in almost total omission of any reference in their bulletins to any reverses presumably suffered by the Allies. Ministry of Information probably responsible for this, and cannot help wondering what its functions *really* are. Shall perhaps discover this if proffered

[1] British Broadcasting Corporation.

[35]

services, recently placed at Ministry's disposal by myself, should be accepted.

Say as much to Aunt Blanche, who replies—a little extravagantly—that she only wishes they would put me in charge of the whole thing. Am quite unable to echo this aspiration and in any case am aware that it will not be realised.

Pay parting call on Our Vicar's Wife, and find her very pale but full of determination and not to be daunted by the fact that she has no maids at all. Members of the Women's Institute have, she says, come to the rescue and several of them taking it in turns to come up and Give a Hand in the Mornings, which is, we agree, what is really needed everywhere. They have also formed a Mending Pool—which is, Our Vicar's Wife says, wartime expression denoting ordinary old-fashioned working-party.

Doubt has been cast on the possibility of continuing W. I. Monthly Meetings but this dispersed by announcement, said to have come from the Lord Privy Seal no less, that they are to be continued. Mrs. F. from the mill—our secretary—has undertaken to inform all members that the Lord Privy Seal says that we are to go on with our meetings just the same and so it will be all right.

Enquire after Rectory evacuees—can see two of them chasing the cat in garden—and Our Vicar's Wife says Oh, well, there they are, poor little things, and one mother has written to her husband to come and fetch her and the child away but he hasn't done so, for which Our Vicar's Wife doesn't blame him—and the other mother seems to be settling down and has offered to do the washing-up. The child who had fits is very well-behaved and the other two will, suggests Our Vicar's Wife optimistically, come into line presently. She then tells me how they went out and picked up fir cones and were unfortunately inspired to throw them down lavatory pan to see if they floated, with subsequent jamming of the drain.

Still, everything is all right and both she and Our Vicar quite feel that nothing at all matters except total destruction of Hitlerism. Applaud her heartily and offer to try to find maid in London and send her down. Meanwhile, has she tried Labour Exchange? She has, but results not good. Only one candidate available for interview, who said that she had hitherto looked after dogs. Particularly sick dogs, with mange. Further enquiries as to her ability to cook only elicited information that she used to cook for the dogs—and Our Vicar's Wife compelled to dismiss application as unsuitable.

Conversation is interrupted by fearful outburst of screams from infant evacuees in garden between whom mysterious feud has suddenly leapt into being, impelling them to fly at one another's throats. Our Vicar's Wife taps on window-pane sharply—to no effect whatever— but assures me that It's Always Happening, and they'll settle down presently, and the mothers will be sure to come out and separate them in a minute.

One of them does so, slaps both combatants heartily, and then leads them, bellowing, indoors.

Can see that Our Vicar's Wife—usually so ready with enlightened theories on upbringing of children, of whom she has none of her own— is so worn-out as to let anybody do anything, and am heartily sorry for her.

Tell her so—she smiles wanly, but repeats

that she will put up with anything so long as Hitler *goes*—and we part affectionately.

Meet several people in the village, and exchange comments on such topics as food-rationing, possible shortage of sugar, and inability ever to go anywhere on proposed petrol allowance. Extraordinary and characteristically English tendency on the part of everybody to go into fits of laughter and say Well, we're all in the same boat, aren't we, and we've got to *show* 'Itler he can't go on like that, haven't we?

Agree that we have, and that we will.

On reaching home Winnie informs me that Mr. Humphrey Holloway is in the drawing-room and wishes to speak to me. Tell her to bring in an extra cup for tea and ask Cook for some chocolate biscuits.

Find H. H.—middle-aged bachelor who has recently bought small bungalow on the Common—exchanging views about Stalin with Aunt Blanche. Neither thinks well of him. Ask Aunt Blanche if she has heard the Four O'clock News —Yes, she has, and there was nothing. Nothing turns out to be that Hitler, speaking yesterday

in Danzig, has declared that Great Britain is
responsible for the war, and that Mr. Chamberlain, speaking to-day in Parliament, has re-
affirmed British determination to redeem Europe
from perpetual fear of Nazi aggression. Thank
Heaven for that, says Aunt Blanche piously,
we've got to fight it out to a finish now, and
would Mr. Holloway very kindly pass her the
brown bread-and-butter.

It turns out that H. H. has heard I am going
up to London to-morrow and would I care to
go up with him in his car, as he wishes to offer
his services to the Government, but has been
three times rejected for the Army owing to
myopia and hay-fever. The roads, he asserts,
will very likely be blocked with military transport, especially in Salisbury neighbourhood,
but he proposes—if I agree—to start at seven
o'clock in the morning.

Accept gratefully, and enquire in general
terms how local evacuees are getting on? Better, returns H. H. guardedly, than in some parts
of the country, from all he hears. Recent warning broadcast from B.B.C.[1] regarding prob-

[1] British Broadcasting Corporation.

ability of London children gathering and eating deadly nightshade from the hedges, though doubtless well-intended, has had disastrous effect on numerous London parents, who have hurriedly reclaimed their offspring from this perilous possibility.

Point out that real deadly nightshade is exceedingly rare in any hedge but Aunt Blanche says compassionately that probably the B.B.C. doesn't know this, error on the subject being extremely common. Am rather taken aback at this attitude towards the B.B.C. and can see that H. H. is too, but Aunt Blanche quite unmoved and merely asks whether the blackberry jelly is home-made. Adds that she will willingly help to make more if Marigold, Margery and Doreen Fitzgerald will pick the blackberries.

Accept this gratefully and hope it is not unpatriotic to couple it with a plea that Aunt Blanche will neither make, nor allow Cook to make, any marrow jam—as can perfectly remember its extreme and universal unpopularity in 1916, '17 and '18.

Robin, due to return to school to-morrow, comes in late and embarks on discussion with

H. H. concerning probability or otherwise of repeal of the arms embargo in the U.S.A. This becomes so absorbing that when H. H. takes his leave, Robin offers to accompany him in order to continue it, and does so.

Aunt Blanche says that Robin is a very dear boy and it seems only yesterday that he was running about in his little yellow smock and look at him now! My own thoughts have been following very similar lines, but quite realise that morale—so important to us all at present juncture—will be impaired if I dwell upon them for even two minutes. Suggest instead that Children's Hour now considerably overdue, and we might play Ludo with little evacuees, to which Aunt Blanche at once assents, but adds that she can play just as well while going on with her knitting.

Towards seven o'clock Robert returns from A.R.P.[1] office—large, ice-cold room kindly lent by Guild of Congregational Ladies—is informed of suggestion that H. H. should motor me to London, to which he replies with a reminder that I must take my gas-mask, and, after

[1] Air Raid Precautions.

a long silence, tells me that he has a new helper in the office who is driving him mad. She is, he tells me in reply to urgent questioning, a Mrs. Wimbush, and she has a swivel eye.

As Robert adds nothing to this, feel constrained to ask What Else?

Elicit by degrees that Mrs. Wimbush is giving her services voluntarily, that she types quickly and accurately, is thoroughly efficient, never makes a mistake, arrives with the utmost punctuality, and always knows where to find everything.

Nevertheless, Robert finds her intolerable.

Am very sorry for him and say that I can quite understand it—which I can—and refer to Dr. Fell. Evening spent in remembering quantities of things that I meant to tell Cook, Winnie, Aunt Blanche and the gardener about proper conduct of the house in my absence.

Also write long letter to mother of Marigold and Margery, begging her to come down and see them when she can, and assuring her of the well-being of both. (Just as I finish this, Robin informs me that Marigold was sick in the bathroom after her supper, but decide not to re-open letter on that account.) Make all farewells overnight and assert that I shall leave the house noiselessly without disturbing anyone at dawn.

September 22nd.—Ideal of noiseless departure not wholly realised (never really thought it would be); as Robert appears in dressing-gown and pyjamas to carry my suitcase downstairs for me, Cook, from behind partially-closed kitchen-passage door, thrusts a cup of tea into my hand, and dog Benjy, evidently under impression that I am about to take him for an early walk, capers joyfully round and round, barking.

Moreover, Humphrey Holloway, on stroke of seven precisely, drives up to hall door by no means inaudibly.

Say goodbye to Robert—promise to let him hear the minute I know about my job—snatch up gas-mask in horrible little cardboard container, and go. Have extraordinarily strong premonition that I shall never see home again. (Have often had this before.) Humphrey H. and I exchange good-mornings, he asks, in reference to my luggage, if that is All, and we drive away.

Incredibly lovely September morning, with white mists curling above the meadows and cobwebs glittering in the hedges, and am reminded of Pip's departure from the village early in the morning in *Great Expectations*. Ask H. H. if he knows it and he says Yes, quite well—but adds that he doesn't remember a word of it. Subject is allowed to drop. Roads are empty, car flies along and we reach Mere at hour which admits of breakfast and purchase of newspapers. Am, as usual, unable to resist remarkable little column entitled Inside Information in *Daily Sketch*, which has hitherto proved uncannily correct in every forecast made. Should much like to know how this is achieved.

Likewise buy and read *The Times*, excellent in its own way but, as H. H. and I agree, quite a different cup of tea. Resume car again and drive off with equal speed. H. H. makes no idle conversation, which is all to the good, and am forced to the conclusion that men, in this respect, far better than women. When he eventually breaks silence, it is to suggest that we should drive round by Stonehenge and have a look at it. The sight of Stonehenge, thinks H.

H., will help us to realise the insignificance of our own troubles.

Am delighted to look at Stonehenge and theoretically believe H. H. to be right, but am practically certain, from past experience, that neither Stonehenge nor any other monument, however large and ancient, will really cause actual present difficulties to vanish into instant nothingness. (*Note:* Theory one thing, real life quite another. Do not say anything of this aloud.)

Overtake the military, soon afterwards, sitting in heaps on large Army lorries and all looking very youthful. They wave, and laugh, and sing "We'll Hang Out the Washing on the Siegfried Line" and "South of the Border."

Wave back again, and am dreadfully reminded of 1914. In order to dispel this, owing to importance of keeping morale in good repair, talk to Humphrey H. about—as usual—evacuees, and we exchange anecdotes.

H. tells me of rich woman who is reported to have said that the secret of the whole thing is to Keep the Classes Separate and that High School children must never, on any account, be asked to sit down to meals with Secondary

School children. Am appalled, and agree heartily with his assertion that if we get a Bolshevik régime over here, it will be no more than some of us deserve.

I then tell H. H. about builder in South Wales who received three London school children and complained that two cried every night and the third was a young tough who knocked everything about, and all must be removed or his wife would have immediate nervous breakdown. Weeping infants .accordingly handed over to elderly widow and tough sent off in deep disgrace to share billet of teacher. Two days later—it may have been more, but two days sounds well—widow appears before billeting officer, with all three evacuees, and declares her intention of keeping the lot. The tough, in tears, is behind her pushing juniors in a little go-cart. No further complaints heard from either side.

H. H. seems touched, and says with great emphasis that that's exactly what he means. (This passes muster at the time, but on thinking it over, can see no real justification for the assertion.)

Interchange of stories interrupted by roarings

overhead, and I look up with some horror at wingless machine flying low and presenting appearance as of giant species of unwholesome-looking insect. H. H.—association of ideas quite unmistakable—abruptly observes that he hopes I have remembered to bring my gas-mask. Everyone up here, he asserts, will be wearing them.

Does he mean *wearing* them, I ask, or only just wearing them?

He means just wearing them, slung over one shoulder. Sure enough shortly afterwards pass group of school children picking blackberries in the hedges, each one with little square box—looking exactly like picnic lunch—hanging down behind.

After this, gas-mask absolutely universal and perceive that my own cardboard container, slung on string, is quite *démodé* and must be supplied with more decorative case. Great variety of colour and material evidently obtainable, from white waterproof to gay red and blue checks.

Traffic still very scarce, even when proceeding up Putney Hill, and H. H. says he's never

Hawking gas-mask cases.

seen anything like it and won't mind driving
into London at all, although he usually stops
just outside, but this is all as simple as possible.

Very soon afterwards he dashes briskly down
one-way street and is turned back by the police
into Trafalgar Square, round which we drive
three times before H. H. gets into right line of
traffic for the Strand. He also makes abortive
effort to shoot direct down Buckingham Street
—likewise one-way—but am able to head him
off in time.

Strand has very little traffic, but men along
edges of pavement are energetically hawking
gas-mask cases, and also small and inferior-
looking document evidently of facetious nature,
purporting to be Last Will and Testament of
Adolf Hitler.

Am reminded of cheap and vulgar conun-
drum, brought home by Robin, as to What Hitler said when he fell through the bed. Reply
is: At last I'm in Poland. Dismiss immediately
passing fancy of repeating this to Humphrey
Holloway, and instead make him civil speech
of gratitude for having brought me to my door.

[49]

In return he extracts my suitcase, and gas-mask from car, declares that it has been a pleasure, and drives off.

September 23rd.—Installed in Buckingham Street top-floor flat, very nicely furnished and Rose's cousin's taste in pictures—reproductions of Frith's Derby Day, Ramsgate Sands and Paddington Station—delight me and provide ideal escape from present-day surroundings. Foresee that much time will be spent sitting at writing-table looking at them, instead of writing. (*Query:* Should this be viewed as sheer waste of time, or reasonable relaxation? *Answer:* Reminiscent of Robert—can only be that It Depends.)

This thought takes me straight to telephone, so as to put through trunk-call home. Operator tells me austerely that full fee of half-a-crown will be charged for three minutes, and I cancel call. Ring up Rose instead, at cost of two-pence only, and arrange to meet her for lunch on Wednesday.

Is she, I enquire, very busy?

No, not at present. But she is Standing By. Gather from tone in which she says this that it will be useless to ask if she can think of anything for me to do, so ring off.

Ministry of Information will no doubt be in better position to suggest employment.

Meanwhile, am under oath to Aunt Blanche to go down to Adelphi underworld and look up Serena Fiddlededee, and also—has said Aunt Blanche—let her know if Pussy Winter-Gammon has come to her senses yet. Just as I am departing on this errand, occupier of ground-floor offices emerges and informs me that he is owner of the house, and has never really approved of the sub-letting of top flat. Still, there it is, it's done now. But he thinks it right that I should be in possession of following facts:

This house is three hundred years old and will burn like tinder if—am not sure he didn't say *when*—incendiary bomb falls on the roof.

It is well within official danger zone.

The basement is quite as unsafe as the rest of the house.

The stairs are extremely steep, narrow and winding, and anyone running down them in a hurry in the night would have to do so in pitch darkness and would almost certainly end up with a broken neck at the bottom.

If I choose to sleep in the house, I shall be quite alone there. (Can well understand this, after all he has been saying about its disadvantages.)

Rather more hopeful note is struck when he continues to the effect that there *is* an air-raid shelter within two minutes' walk, and it will accommodate a hundred and fifty people.

I undertake to make myself instantly familiar with its whereabouts, and to go there without fail in the event of an air-raid alarm.

Conversation concludes with the owner's assurance that whatever I do is done on my own responsibility, in which I acquiesce, and my departure into Buckingham Street.

Spirits rather dashed until I glance up and see entire sky peppered with huge silver balloons, which look lovely. Cannot imagine why they have never been thought of before and used for purely decorative purposes.

Find entrance to Adelphi underground organisation strongly guarded by two pallid-looking A.R.P.[1] officials to whom I show pass, furnished by Aunt Blanche, *via*—presumably —Miss Serena Fiddlededee. Perceive that I am getting into the habit of thinking of her by this name and must take firm hold of myself if I am not to make use of it when we meet face to face.

Descend lower and lower down concrete-paved slope—classical parallel here with Proserpina's excursion into Kingdom of Pluto—and emerge under huge vaults full of ambulances ranged in rows, with large cars sandwiched between.

Trousered women are standing and walking about in every direction, and great number of men with armlets. Irrelevant reflection here to the effect that this preponderance of masculine society, so invaluable at any social gathering, is never to be seen on ordinary occasions.

Rather disquieting notice written in red chalk on matchboard partitions, indicates directions to be taken by Decontaminated Women, Walking Cases, Stretcher-bearers and others—but am

[1] Air Raid Precautions.

presently relieved by perceiving arrow with inscription: To No. 1 Canteen—where I accordingly proceed. Canteen is large room, insufficiently lit, with several long tables, a counter with urns and plates, kitchen behind, and at least one hundred and fifty people standing and sitting about, all looking exactly like the people already seen outside.

Wireless is blaring out rather inferior witticisms, gramophone emitting raucous rendering of "We'll Hang Out the Washing on the Siegfried Line" and very vocal game of darts proceeding merrily. Am temporarily stunned, but understand that everybody is only Standing By. Now I come to think of it, am doing so myself.

Atmosphere thick with cigarette smoke and no apparent ventilation anywhere. Noise indescribable. Remember with some horror that Aunt Blanche said everybody was doing twenty-four-hour shifts and sleeping on camp-beds on the premises. Am deeply impressed by this devotion to duty and ask myself if I could possibly do so much. Answer probably No.

Very pretty girl with dark curls—in slacks,

like everybody else—screams into my ear, in order to make herself heard: Am I looking for anyone? Should like to ask for Serena, whom I have always thought charming, but impossible to shriek back: Have you anybody here called Serena Fiddlededee?—name still a complete blank. Am consequently obliged to enquire for my only other acquaintance in the underworld, old Mrs. Winter-Gammon—not charming at all.

Very pretty girl giggles and says Oh, do I mean Granny Bo-Peep? which immediately strikes me as most brilliant nickname ever invented and entirely suited to Mrs. Winter-Gammon. She is at once pointed out, buying Gold Flake cigarettes at Canteen counter, and I look at her with considerable disfavour. Cannot possibly be less than sixty-six, but has put herself into diminutive pair of blue trousers, short-sleeved wool jumper, and wears her hair, which is snow-white, in roguish mop of curls bolt upright all over her head. Old Mrs. W.-G. stands about five foot high, and is very slim and active, and now chatting away merrily to about a dozen ambulance men.

Pretty girl informs me very gloomily that Granny Bo-Peep is the Sunbeam of the Adelphi. Am filled with horror and say that I made a mistake, I don't really want to see her after all. Mrs. W.-G. has, however, seen me and withdrawal becomes impossible. She positively dances up to me, and carols out her astonishment and delight at my presence. Am disgusted at hearing myself replying with cordiality amounting to enthusiasm.

She enquires affectionately after Aunt Blanche, and I say that she sent her love—cannot be *absolutely* certain that she didn't really say something of the kind—and Mrs. W.-G. smiles indulgently and says Poor dear old Blanche, she'll be better and happier out of it all in the country, and offers to show me round.

We proceed to inspect ambulances—ready day and night—motor cars, all numbered and marked Stretcher Parties—Red Cross Station —fully equipped and seems thoroughly well organised, which is more than can be said for Women's Rest-room, packed with uncomfortable-looking little camp-beds of varying de-

Mrs. W.-G. simply dances up.

signs, tin helmets slung on hooks round match-boarded walls, two upright wooden chairs and large printed sheet giving Instructions in the event of an Air-raid Warning. Several women —still in trousers and jumpers—huddle exhaustedly on the camp-beds, and atmosphere blue with cigarette smoke.

Noise is, if possible, greater in Rest-room than anywhere else in the building as it is situated between Canteen and ambulance station, where every now and then all engines are started up and run for five minutes. Canteen wireless and gramophone both clearly audible, also rather amateurish rendering of "South of the Border" on unlocated, but not distant, piano.

Screech out enquiry as to whether anyone can ever manage to sleep in here, and Mrs. W.-G. replies Yes, indeed, it *is* a comfort to have Winston in the Cabinet. This takes me outside the door, and am able to repeat enquiry which is, this time, audible.

Mrs. W.-G.—very sunny—assures me that the young ones sleep through everything. As for old campaigners like herself, what does it matter? She went through the last war practically side by side with Our Boys behind the lines, as near to the trenches as she could get. Lord Kitchener on more than one occasion said to her: Mrs. Winter-Gammon, if only the regulations allowed me to do so, *you* are the person whom I should recommend for the Victoria Cross. That, of course, says Mrs. W.-G. modestly, was nonsense—(should think so indeed)—but Lord K. had ridiculous weakness for her. Personally, she never could understand what people meant by calling him a woman-hater. Still, there it was. She supposes that she *was* rather a privileged person in the war.

Have strong inclination to ask if she means the Crimean War, but enquire instead what work she is engaged on here and now. Well, at the moment, she is Standing By, affirms Mrs. W.-G. lighting cigarette and sticking it into one corner of her mouth at rakish angle. She will, when the emergency arises, drive a car. She had originally volunteered to drive an ambulance but proved—hee-hee-hee—to be too tiny. Her feet wouldn't reach the pedals and her hands wouldn't turn the wheel.

Am obliged, on Mrs. W.-G.'s displayal of what look to me like four particularly frail claws, to admit the justice of this.

She adds that, in the meantime, she doesn't mind what she does. She just gives a hand here, there and everywhere, and tries to jolly everybody along. People sometimes say to her that she will destroy herself, she gives out so much all the time—but to this her only reply is: What does it matter if she does? Why, just nothing at all!

Am wholly in agreement, and much inclined to say so. Ruffianly-looking man in red singlet, khaki shorts and armlet goes by and Mrs. W.-G. calls out merrily: Hoo-hoo! to which he makes no reply whatever, and she tells me that he is one of the demolition squad and a dear boy, a very special friend of hers, and she loves pulling his leg.

Am unsympathetically silent, but old Mrs. W.-G. at once heaps coals of fire on my head by offering me coffee and a cigarette from the Canteen, and we sit down at comparatively empty table to strains of "The Siegfried Line" from gramophone and "In the Shadows" from

the wireless. Coffee is unexpectedly good and
serves to support me through merry chatter of
Granny Bo-Peep, who has more to say of her
own war service, past and present.

Coma comes on, partly due to airless and
smoke-laden atmosphere, partly to mental exhaustion, and am by no means clear whether
Mrs. W.-G.'s reminiscences are not now taking
us back to Peninsular War or possibly even
Wars of the Roses.

Am sharply roused by series of shrill blasts
from powerful whistle: Mrs. W.-G. leaps up
like a (small) chamois and says, It's a mock
Air-raid alarm, only for practice—I'm not to
be frightened—which I wasn't, and shouldn't
dream of being, and anyhow shouldn't show it
if I was—and she must be off to her post. She
then scampers away, tossing her curls as she
goes, darts out at one door and darts in again
at another—curls now extinguished under tin-
hat—pulling on leather jacket as she runs.
Quantities of other people all do the same,
though with less celerity.

Can hear engines, presumably of ambulances,
being started and temporarily displacing gramophone and wireless.

Spirited game of darts going on in one corner amongst group already pointed out to me by old Mrs. W.-G. as those dear, jolly boys of the Demolition Squad, comes to an abrupt end, and only Canteen workers remain, conversing earnestly behind plates of buns, bananas and chocolate biscuits. Can plainly hear one of them telling another that practically every or-ganisation in London is turning voluntary workers away by the hundred, as there is nothing for them to do. *At present*, she adds darkly. Friend returns that it is the same story all over the country. Land Army alone has had to choke off several thousand applicants—and as for civil aviation ——

Before I can learn what is happening about civil aviation—but am prepared to bet that it's being told to Stand By—I am accosted by Aunt Blanche's friend, Serena Fiddlededee. She is young and rather pretty, with enormous round eyes, and looks as if she might—at out-side estimate—weigh seven and a half stone. Trousers brown, which is a relief after so much navy blue, jumper scarlet and leather-jacket orange. General effect gay and decorative. Quite idle fancy flits through my mind of adopting

[61]

similar attire and achieving similar result
whilst at the selfsame moment the voice of common sense informs me that a considerable number of years separates me from Serena and the
wearing of bright colours alike. (Opening here
for interesting speculation: Do not all women
think of themselves as still looking exactly as
they did at twenty-five, whilst perfectly aware
that as many years again have passed over their
heads?)

Serena astonishes me by expressing delight at
seeing me, and asks eagerly if I have come to
join up. Can only say that I have and I haven't.
Am more than anxious to take up work for
King and Country but admit that, so far, every
attempt to do so has been met with discourage-
ment.

Serena says Yes, yes—she knows it's like that
—and she herself wouldn't be here now if she
hadn't dashed round to the Commandant two
days before war was declared at all and offered
to scrub all the floors with disinfectant. After
that, they said she might drive one of the cars.

And has she?

Serena sighs, and rolls her enormous eyes,
and admits that she was once sent to fetch the

Commandant's laundry from Streatham. All the other drivers were most fearfully jealous, because none of *them* have done anything at all except Stand By.

I enquire why Serena isn't taking part in the mock air-raid, and she says negligently that she is off duty just now but hasn't yet summoned up energy to go all the way to Belsize Park where she inconveniently lives. She adds that she is rather sorry, in a way, to miss the test, because the last one they had was quite exciting. A girl called Moffat or Muffet, was the first driver in the line and had, Serena thinks, only just passed her "L" test and God alone knows how she'd done that. And instead of driving up the ramp, round the corner and out into the Adelphi, she'd shot straight forward, missed the Commandant by millimetres, knocked down part of the structure of Gentlemen and reversed onto the bumpers of the car behind. You could, avers Serena, absolutely *see* the battle-bowlers rising from the heads of the four stretcher-bearers inside the car. Moffat or Muffet, shortly after this dramatic performance, was sacked.

Serena then offers me coffee and a cigarette.

I reply, though gratefully, that I have already had both and she assures me that this war is really being won on coffee and cigarettes, by women in trousers. Speaking of trousers, have I seen Granny Bo-Peep. Yes, I have. Serena goes off into fits of laughter, and says Really, this war is terribly funny *in its own way*, isn't it? Reply that I see what she means—which I do—and that, so far, it's quite unlike any other war. One keeps on wondering when something is going to happen. Yes, agrees Serena mournfully, and when one says that, everybody looks horrified and asks if one *wants* to be bombed by the Germans and see the Nelson Column go crashing into Trafalgar Square. They never, says Serena in a rather resentful tone, suggest the Albert Hall crashing into Kensington, which for her part she could view with equanimity.

We then refer to Aunt Blanche—how she stood Granny Bo-Peep as long as she did is a mystery to Serena—the evacuees at home—how lucky I am to have really nice ones. No lice? interpolates Serena, sounding astonished. Certainly no lice. They're not in the *least* like that. Charming children, very well brought-up

[64]

—sometimes I am inclined to think, better brought up than Robin and Vicky—to which Serena civilly ejaculates Impossible!

Canteen comes under discussion—very well run and no skin on the cocoa, which Serena thinks is *the* test. Open day and night because workers are on twenty-four-hour shift. Enquire of Serena whether she ever gets any sleep in the Rest-room, and she replies rather doubtfully that she thinks she does, sometimes. On the whole most of her sleeping is done at home. She has four Jewish Refugees in her flat—very, very nice ones, but too many of them—and they cook her the most excellent Viennese dishes. Originally she had only one refugee, but gradually a mother, a cousin, and a little boy have joined the party, Serena doesn't know how. They all fit into one bedroom and the kitchen and she herself has remaining bedroom and sitting-room, only she's never there.

Suggest that she should make use of Buckingham Street flat whenever convenient, and she accepts and says may she go there immediately and have a bath?

Certainly.

[65]

We proceed at once to Rest-room for Serena to collect her things, and she shows me horrible-looking little canvas affair about three inches off the floor, swung on poles like inferior sort of hammock. Is that her bed?

Yes, says Serena, and she has shown it to a doctor friend who has condemned it at sight, with rather strangely-worded observation that any bed of that shape is always more or less fatal in the long run, as it throws the kidneys on the bum.

Conduct Serena to top-storey flat, present her with spare latchkey and beg her to come in when she likes and rest on properly constructed divan, which presumably is not open to similar objection.

Am touched when she assures me that I am an angel and have probably saved her life.

Wish I could remember whether I have ever heard her surname, and if so, what it is.

September 23rd.—Postcard from Our Vicar who writes because he feels he ought, in view of recent conversation, to let me know that he has had a letter from a friend in Northumberland on whom two evacuated teachers are billeted, both of whom are *very nice indeed*. Make beds, and play with children, and have offered to dig potatoes. It is a satisfaction, adds Our Vicar across one corner, to know that we were mistaken in saying that everyone complained of the teachers. There are evidently exceptions.

Think well of Our Vicar for this, and wonder if anyone will ever say that mothers, in some cases, are also satisfactory inmates.

Should doubt it.

Spend large part of the day asking practically everybody I can think of, by telephone or letter, if they can suggest a war job for me.

Most of them reply that they are engaged in similar quest on their own account.

Go out into Trafalgar Square and see gigantic poster on Nelson's plinth asking me what form MY service is taking.

Other hoardings of London give equally prominent display to such announcements as that 300,000 Nurses are wanted, 41,000 Ambulance Drivers, and 500,000 Air-raid Wardens. Get into touch with Organisations requiring these numerous volunteers, and am told that

queue five and a half miles long is already be-
sieging their doors.

Ring up influential man at B.B.C.[1]—name
given me by Sir W. Frobisher as being dear
old friend of his—and influential man tells me
in tones of horror that they have a list of really
first-class writers and speakers whom they can
call upon at any moment—which, I gather, they
have no intention of doing—and really couldn't
possibly make any use of me whatever. At the
same time, of course, I can always feel I'm
Standing By.

I say Yes, indeed, and ring off.

Solitary ray of light comes from Serena
Fiddlededee whom I hear in bathroom—on
door of which she has pinned paper marked
ENGAGED—at unnatural hour of 2 P.M. and
who emerges in order to say that *until* I start
work at the Ministry of Information, she thinks
the Adelphi Canteen might be glad of occasional help, if voluntary, and given on night-
shift.

Pass over reference to Ministry of Information and at once agree to go and offer assistance

[1] British Broadcasting Corporation.

at Canteen. Serena declares herself delighted, and offers to introduce me there to-night.

Meanwhile, why not go and see Brigadier Pinflitton, said to be important person in A.R.P.[1] circles? Serena knows him well, and will ring up and say that I am coming and that he will do well to make sure of my assistance before I am snapped up elsewhere.

I beg Serena to modify this last improbable adjuration, but admit that I should be glad of introduction to Brigadier P. if there is the slightest chance of his being able to tell me of something I can do. What does Serena think?

Serena thinks there's almost certain to be a fire-engine or something that I could drive, or perhaps I might decontaminate someone— which leads her on to an enquiry about my gas-mask. How, she wishes to know, do I get on inside it? Serena herself always feels as if she must faint after wearing it for two seconds. She thinks one ought to practise sitting in it in the evenings sometimes.

Rather unalluring picture is conjured up by this, but admit that Serena may be right, and

[1] Air Raid Precautions.

I suggest supper together one evening, followed by sessions in our respective gas-masks.

We can, I say, listen to Sir Walford Davies. Serena says That would be lovely, and offers to obtain black paper for windows of flat, and put it up for me with drawing-pins.

Meanwhile she will do what she can about Brigadier Pinflitton, but wiser to write than to ring up as he is deaf as a post.

September 25th.—No summons from Brigadier Pinflitton, the Ministry of Information, the B.B.C.[1] or anybody else.

Letter from Felicity Fairmead enquiring if she could come and help me, as she is willing to do anything and is certain that I must be fearfully busy.

Reply-paid telegram from Rose asking if I know any influential person on the British Medical Council to whom she could apply for post.

Letter from dear Robin, expressing concern lest I should be over-working, and anxiety to know exactly what form my exertions on behalf of the nation are taking.

Tremendous scene of reunion—not of my

[1] British Broadcasting Corporation.

seeking—takes place in underworld between myself and Granny Bo-Peep, cantering up at midnight for cup of coffee and cigarettes. What, she cries, am I here again? Now, that's what she calls setting a *real* example.

Everyone within hearing looks at me with loathing and I explain that I am doing nothing whatever.

Old Mrs. W.-G., unmoved, goes on to say that seeing me here reminds her of coffee-stall run by herself at the Front in nineteen-fourteen. The boys loved it, she herself loved it, Lord Roberts loved it. Ah, well, Mrs. W.-G. is an old woman now and has to content herself with trotting about in the background doing what she can to cheer up the rest of the world.

Am sorry to say that Demolition Squad, Stretcher-bearers and Ambulance men evince greatest partiality for Mrs. W.-G. and gather round her in groups.

They are, says Serena, a low lot—the other night two of them had a fight and an ambulance man who went to separate them emerged bitten to the bone.

Should be delighted to hear further revelations, but supper rush begins and feel that I had better withdraw.

September 27th.—Day pursues usual routine, so unthinkable a month ago, now so familiar, and continually recalling early Novels of the Future by H. G. Wells—now definitely established as minor prophet. Have very often wondered why all prophecies so invariably of a disturbing nature, predicting unpleasant state of affairs all round. Prophets apparently quite insensible to any brighter aspects of the future.

Ring up five more influential friends between nine and twelve to ask if they know of any national work I can undertake. One proves to be on duty as L.C.C.[1] ambulance driver—at which I am very angry and wonder how on earth she managed to get the job—two more reply that I am the tenth person at least to ask this and that they don't know of anything whatever for me, and the remaining two assure me that I must just *wait*, and in time I shall be told what to do.

Ask myself rhetorically whether it was for this that I left home?

[1] London County Council.

Conscience officiously replies that I left home partly because I had no wish to spend the whole of the war in doing domestic work, partly because I felt too cut-off owing to distance between Devonshire and London, and partly from dim idea that London will be more central if I wish to reach Robin or Vicky in any emergency.

Meet Rose for luncheon. She says that she has offered her services to every hospital in London without success. The Hospitals, says Rose gloomily, are all fully staffed, and the beds are all empty, and nobody is allowed to go in however ill they are, and the medical staff goes to bed at ten o'clock every night and isn't called till eleven next morning because they haven't anything to do. The nurses, owing to similar inactivity, are all quarrelling amongst themselves and throwing the splints at one another's heads.

I express concern but no surprise, having heard much the same thing repeatedly in the course of the last three weeks. Tell Rose in return that I am fully expecting to be offered employment of great national importance by

[73]

the Government at any moment. Can see by Rose's expression that she is not in the least taken in by this. She enquires rather sceptically if I have yet applied for work as voluntary helper on night-shift at Serena's canteen, and I reply with quiet dignity that I shall do so directly I can get anybody to attend to me.

Rose, at this, laughs heartily, and I feel strongly impelled to ask whether the war has made her hysterical—but restrain myself. We drink quantities of coffee, and Rose tells me what she thinks about the Balkans, Stalin's attitude, the chances of an air-raid over London within the week, and the probable duration of the war. In reply I give her my considered opinion regarding the impregnability or otherwise of the Siegfried Line, the neutrality of America, Hitler's intentions with regard to Rumania, and the effect of the petrol rationing on this country as a whole.

We then separate with mutual assurances of letting one another know if we Hear of Anything. In the meanwhile, says Rose rather doubtfully, do I remember the Blowfields? Sir Archibald Blowfield is something in the

[74]

Ministry of Information, and it might be worth
while ringing them up.

I do ring them up in the course of the afternoon, and Lady Blowfield—voice sounds melancholy over the telephone—replies that of course
she remembers me well, we met at Valescure in
the dear old days. Have never set foot in Valescure in my life, but allow this to pass, and explain that my services as lecturer, writer, or
even shorthand typist, are entirely at the disposal of my country if only somebody will be
good enough to utilise them.

Lady Blowfield emits a laugh—saddest
sound I think I have ever heard—and replies
that thousands and thousands of highly-quali-
fied applicants are waiting in a queue outside
her husband's office. In *time*, no doubt, they will
be needed, but at present there is Nothing,
Nothing, Nothing! Unspeakably hollow effect
of these last words sends my morale practically
down to zero, but I rally and thank her very
much. (What for?)

Have I tried the Land Army? enquires Lady
Blowfield.

No, I haven't. If the plough boots, smock

[75]

and breeches are indicated, something tells me
that I should be of very little use to the Land
Army.

Well, says Lady Blowfield with a heavy
sigh, she's terribly, terribly sorry. There seems
nothing for anybody to do, really, except wait
for the bombs to rain down upon their heads.

Decline absolutely to subscribe to this view,
and enquire after Sir Archibald.

Oh, Archibald is killing himself. Slowly but
surely. He works eighteen hours a day, Sundays and all, and neither eats nor sleeps.

Then why, I urge, not let me come and help
him, and set him free for an occasional meal at
least. But to this Lady Blowfield replies that I
don't understand at all. There will be work for
us all eventually—provided we are not Wiped
Out instantly—but for the moment we must
wait. I enquire rather peevishly how long, and
she returns that the war, whatever some people
may say, is quite likely to go on for years and
years. Archibald, personally, has estimated the
probable duration at exactly twenty-two years
and six months. Feel that if I listen to Lady
Blowfield for another moment I shall probably
shoot myself, and ring off.

Just as I am preparing to listen to the Budget announcement on the Six O'clock News, telephone rings and I feel convinced that I am to be sent for by someone at a moment's notice, to do something, somewhere, and dash to the receiver.

Call turns out to be from old friend Cissie Crabbe, asking if I can find her a war job. Am horrified at hearing myself replying that in time, no doubt, we shall all be needed, but for the moment there is nothing to do but *wait*.

Budget announcement follows and is all that one could have foreseen, and more. Evolve hasty scheme for learning to cook and turning home into a boarding-house after the war, as the only possible hope of remaining there at all.

September 28th.—Go through now habitual performance of pinning up brown paper over the windows and drawing curtains before departing to underworld. Night is as light as possible, and in any case only two minutes' walk.

Just as I arrive, Serena emerges in trousers, little suède jacket and tin hat, beneath which her eyes look positively gigantic. She tells me she is off duty for an hour, and suggests that we should go and drink coffee somewhere.

[77]

We creep along the street, feeling for edges of the pavement with our feet, and eventually reach a Lyons Corner House, entrance to which is superbly buttressed by mountainous stacks of sandbags with tiny little aperture dramatically marked "In" and "Out" on piece of unpainted wood. Serena points out that this makes it all look much more war-like than if "In" and "Out" had been printed in the ordinary way on cardboard.

She then takes off her tin hat, shows me her new gas-mask container—very elegant little vermilion affair with white spots, in waterproof—and utters to the effect that, for her part, she has worked it all out whilst Standing By and finds that her income tax will *definitely* be in excess of her income, which simplifies the whole thing. Ask if she minds, and Serena says No, not in the least, and orders coffee.

She tells me that ever since I last saw her she has been, as usual, sitting about in the underworld, but that this afternoon everybody was told to attend a lecture on the treatment of Shock. The first shock that Serena herself anticipates is the one we shall all experience when

[78]

we get something to do. Tell her of my conversation over the telephone with Lady Blowfield and Serena says Pah! to the idea of a twenty-two-year war and informs me that she was taken out two days ago to have a drink by a very nice man in the Air Force, and he said Six months at the very outside—and he ought to know.

We talk about the Canteen—am definitely of opinion that I shall never willingly eat sausage-and-mashed again as long as I live—the income tax once more—the pronouncement of the cleaner of the Canteen that the chief trouble with Hitler is that he's such a *fidget*—and the balloon barrage, which, Serena assures me in the tone of one giving inside information, is all to come down in November. (When I indignantly ask why, she is unable to substantiate the statement in any way.)

We smoke cigarettes, order more coffee, and I admit to Serena that I don't think I've ever really understood about the balloons. Serena offers to explain—which I think patronising but submit to—and I own to rather fantastic idea as to each balloon containing an observer,

[79]

more or less resembling the look-out in crow's
nest of old-fashioned sailing vessel. This subsequently discarded on being told, probably by
Serena herself, that invisible network of wires
connects the balloons to one another, all wires
being electrified and dealing instant death to
approaching enemy aircraft.

Serena now throws over electrified-wire
theory completely, and says Oh no, it isn't like
that at all. Each balloon is attached to a huge
lorry below, in which sits a Man, perpetually on
guard. She has actually seen one of the lorries,
in front of the Admiralty, with the Man inside
sitting reading a newspaper, and another man
close by to keep him company, cooking something on a little oil-stove.

Shortly afterwards Serena declares that she
must go—positively *must*.

She then remains where she is for twenty
minutes more, and when she does go, leaves her
gas-mask behind her and we have to go back
for it. The waiter who produces it congratulates
Serena on having her name inside the case.
Not a day, he says in an offhand manner, passes
without half a dozen gas-masks being left be-

hind by their owners and half of them have no name, and the other half just have "Bert" or "Mum" or "Our Stanley," which, he says, doesn't take you anywhere at all.

He is thanked by Serena, whom I then escort to entrance of underworld, where she trails away swinging her tin helmet and assuring me that she will probably get the sack for being late if anybody sees her.

September 30th.—Am invited by Serena to have tea at her flat, Jewish refugees said to be spending day with relations at Bromley. Not, says Serena, that she wants to get rid of them— she likes them—but their absence does make more room in the flat.

On arrival it turns out that oldest of the refugees has changed his mind about Bromley and remained behind. He says he has a letter to write.

Serena introduces me—refugee speaks no English and I no German and we content ourselves with handshakes, bows, smiles and more handshakes. He looks patriarchal and dignified, sitting over electric fire in large great-coat.

Serena says he feels the cold. They all feel

the cold. She can't bear to contemplate what it will be like for them when the cold really begins—which it hasn't done at all so far—and she has already piled upon their beds all the blankets she possesses. On going to buy others at large Store, she is told that all blankets have been, are being, and will be, bought by the Government and that if by any extraordinary chance one or two *do* get through, they will cost five times more than ever before.

Beg her not to be taken in by this for one moment and quote case of Robert's aunt, elderly maiden lady living in Chester, who has, since outbreak of war, purchased set of silver dessert-knives, large chiming clock, bolt of white muslin, new rabbit-skin neck-tie and twenty-four lead pencils—none of which she required— solely because she has been told in shops that these will in future be unobtainable. Serena looks impressed and refugee and I shake hands once more.

Serena takes me to her sitting-room, squeezes past two colossal trunks in very small hall, which Serena explains as being luggage of her refugees. The rest of it is in the kitchen and

He feels the cold.

under the beds, except largest trunk of all which couldn't be got beyond ground floor and has had to be left with hall porter.

Four O'clock News on wireless follows. Listeners once more informed of perfect unanimity on all points between French and English Governments. Make idle suggestion to Serena that it would be much more interesting if we were suddenly to be told that there had been several sharp divergences of opinion. And probably much truer too, says Serena cynically, and anyway, if they always agree so perfectly, why meet at all? She calls it waste of time and money.

Am rather scandalised at this, and say so, and Serena immediately declares that she didn't mean a word of it, and produces tea and admirable cakes made by Austrian refugee. Conversation takes the form—extraordinarily prevalent in all circles nowadays—of exchanging rather singular pieces of information, never obtained by direct means but always heard of through friends of friends.

Roughly tabulated, Serena's news is to following effect:

[83]

The whole of the B.B.C.[1] is really functioning from a place in the Cotswolds, and Broadcasting House is full of nothing but sandbags.

A Home for Prostitutes has been evacuated from a danger zone outside London to Aldershot.

(At this I protest, and Serena admits that it was related by young naval officer who has reputation as a wit.)

A large number of war casualties have already reached London, having come up the Thames in barges, and are installed in blocks of empty flats by the river—but nobody knows they're there.

Hitler and Ribbentrop are no longer on speaking terms.

Hitler and Ribbentrop have made it up again.

The Russians are going to turn dog on the Nazis at any moment.

In return for all this, I am in a position to inform Serena:

That the War Office is going to Carnarvon Castle.

A letter has been received in London from a

[1] British Broadcasting Corporation.

[84]

German living in Berlin, with a private message under the stamp saying that a revolution is expected to break out at any minute.

President Roosevelt has been flown over the Siegfried Line and flown back to Washington again, in the strictest secrecy.

The deb. at the canteen, on being offered a marshmallow out of a paper bag, has said: What *is* a marshmallow? (Probably related to a High Court Judge.)

The Russians are determined to assassinate Stalin at the first opportunity.

A woman fainted in the middle of Regent Street yesterday and two stretcher-bearers came to the rescue and put her on the stretcher, then dropped it and fractured both her arms. Serena assures me that in the event of her being injured in any air-raid she has quite decided to emulate Sir Philip Sidney and give everybody else precedence.

Talking of that, would it be a good idea to practise wearing our gas-masks?

Agree, though rather reluctantly, and we accordingly put them on and sit opposite one another in respective armchairs, exchanging sepulchral-sounding remarks from behind talc-and-rubber snouts.

Serena says she wishes to time herself, as she doesn't think she will be able to breathe for more than four minutes at the very most.

Explain that this is all nerves. Gas-masks may be rather warm—(am streaming from every pore)—and perhaps rather uncomfortable, and certainly unbecoming—but any sensible person can breathe inside them for hours.

Serena says I shall be sorry when she goes off into a dead faint.

The door opens suddenly and remaining Austrian refugees, returned early from Bromley, walk in and, at sight presented by Serena and myself are startled nearly out of their senses and enquire in great agitation What is happening.

Remove gas-mask quickly—Serena hasn't fainted at all but is crimson in the face, and hair very untidy—and we all bow and shake hands.

Letter-writing refugee joins us—shakes hands again—and we talk agreeably round tea-table till the letter-motif recurs—they all say they have letters to write, and—presumably final—handshaking closes séance.

Just as I prepare to leave, Serena's bell rings and she says It's J. L. and I'm to wait, because she wants me to meet him.

J. L. turns out to be rather distinguished-looking man, face perfectly familiar to me from *Radio Times* and other periodicals as he is well-known writer and broadcaster. (Wish I hadn't been so obliging about gas-mask, as hair certainly more untidy than Serena's and have not had the sense to powder my nose.)

J. L. is civility itself and pretends to have heard of me often—am perfectly certain he hasn't—and even makes rather indefinite reference to my Work, which he qualifies as well known, but wisely gives conversation another turn immediately without committing himself further.

Serena produces sherry and enquires what J. L. is doing.

Well, J. L. is writing a book.

He is, as a matter of fact, going on with identical book—merely a novel—that he was writing before war began. It isn't that he *wants* to

[87]

do it, or that he thinks anybody else wants him to do it. But he is over military age, and the fourteen different organisations to whom he has offered his services have replied, without exception, that they have far more people already than they know what to do with.

He adds pathetically that authors, no doubt, are very useless people.

Not more so than anybody else, Serena replies. Why can't they be used for propaganda?

J. L. and I—with one voice—assure her that every author in the United Kingdom has had exactly this idea, and has laid it before the Ministry of Information, and has been told in return to Stand By for the present.

In the case of Sir Hugh Walpole, to J. L.'s certain knowledge, a Form was returned on which he was required to state all particulars of his qualifications, where educated, and to which periodicals he has contributed, also names of any books he may ever have had published.

Serena enquires witheringly if they didn't want to know whether the books had been published at Sir H. W.'s own expense, and we all agree that if this is official reaction to Sir H.'s offer, the rest of us need not trouble to make any.

Try to console J. L. with assurance that there is to be a boom in books, as nobody will be able to do anything amusing in the evenings, what with black-out, petrol restrictions, and limitations of theatre and cinema openings, so they will have to fall back on reading.

Realise too late that this not very happily expressed.

J. L. says Yes indeed, and tells me that he finds poetry more helpful than anything else. The Elizabethans for choice. Don't I agree?

Reply at once that I am less familiar with the Elizabethan poets than I should like to be, and hope he may think this means that I know plenty of others. (Am quite unable to recall any poetry at all at the moment, except "How they Brought the Good News from Ghent" and cannot imagine why in the world I should have thought of that.)

Ah, says J. L. very thoughtfully, there is a lot to be said for prose. He personally finds that the Greeks provide him with escapist literature. Plato.

Should not at all wish him to know that *The Fairchild Family* performs the same service for me—but remember with shame that E. M. Forster, in admirable wireless talk, has told us *not* to be ashamed of our taste in reading.

Should like to know if he would apply this to *The Fairchild Family* and can only hope that he would.

Refer to Dickens—compromise here between truth and desire to sound reasonably cultured—but J. L. looks distressed, says Ah yes—really? and changes conversation at once.

Can see that I have dished myself with him for good.

Talk about black-out—Serena alleges that anonymous friend of hers goes out in the dark with extra layer of chalk-white powder on her nose, so as to be seen, and resembles Dong with the Luminous Nose.

J. L. not in the least amused and merely replies that there are little disks on sale, covered with luminous paint, or that pedestrians are now allowed electric torch if pointed downwards, and shrouded in tissue-paper. Serena makes fresh start, and enquires whether he

doesn't know Sir Archibald and Lady Blowfield
—acquaintances of mine.

He does know them—had hoped that Sir A.
could offer him war work—but that neither here
nor there. Lady Blowfield is a charming woman.

I say Yes, isn't she—which is quite contrary
to my real opinion. Moreover, am only distressed at this lapse from truth because aware
that Serena will recognise it as such. Spiritual
and moral degradation well within sight, but
cannot dwell on this now. (*Query:* Is it in any
way true that war very often brings out the best
in civil population? *Answer:* So far as I am
concerned, Not at all.)

Suggestion from Serena that Sir Archibald
and Lady Blowfield both take rather pessimistic
view of international situation causes J. L. to
state it as his considered opinion that no one,
be he whom he may, *no one*, is in a position at
this moment to predict with certainty what the
Future may hold.

Do not like to point out to him that no one
ever has been, and shortly afterwards J. L.
departs, telling Serena that he will ring her up
when he knows any more. (Any more what?)

October 1st.—Am at last introduced by Serena Fiddlededee to underworld Commandant. She is dark, rather good-looking young woman wearing out-size in slacks and leather jacket, using immensely long black cigarette-holder, and writing at wooden trestle-table piled with papers.

Serena—voice sunk to quite unnaturally timid murmur—explains that I am very anxious to make myself of use in any way whatever, while waiting to be summoned by Ministry of Information.

The Commandant—who has evidently heard this kind of thing before—utters short incredulous ejaculation, in which I very nearly join, knowing even better than she does herself how thoroughly well justified it is.

Serena—voice meeker than ever—whispers that I can drive a car if necessary, and have passed my First Aid examination—(hope she isn't going to mention date of this achievement which would take us a long way back indeed)—and am also well used to Home Nursing. Moreover, I can write shorthand and use a typewriter.

Commandant goes on writing rapidly and utters without looking up for a moment—which I think highly offensive. Utterance is to the effect that there are no paid jobs going.

Oh, says Serena, sounding shocked, we never thought of anything like *that*. This is to be voluntary work, and anything in the world, and at any hour.

Commandant—still writing—strikes a bell sharply.

It has been said that the Canteen wants an extra hand, suggests Serena, now almost inaudible. She knows that I should be perfectly willing to work all through the night, or perhaps all day on Sundays, so as to relieve others. And, naturally, voluntary work. To this Commandant —gaze glued to her rapidly-moving pen—mutters something to the effect that voluntary work is all very well ——

Have seldom met more un-endearing personality.

Bell is answered by charming-looking elderly lady wearing overall, and armlet badge inscribed *Messenger*, which seems to me unsuitable.

[93]

Commandant—tones very peremptory indeed
—orders her to Bring the Canteen Time-Sheet.
Grey-haired messenger flies away like the wind.
Cannot possibly have gone more than five yards
from the door before the bell is again struck,
and on her reappearance Commandant says
sharply that she has just asked for Canteen
Time-Sheet. Why hasn't it come?

Obvious reply is that it hasn't come because
only a pair of wings could have brought it in
the time—but no one says this, and Messenger
again departs and can be heard covering the
ground at race-track speed.

Commandant continues to write—says Damn
once, under her breath, as though attacked by
sudden doubt whether war will stop exactly as
and when she has ordained—and drops cigarette
ash all over the table.

Serena looks at me and profanely winks enormous eye.

Bell is once more banged—am prepared to
wager it will be broken before week is out at
this rate. It is this time answered by smart-
looking person in blue trousers and singlet and
admirable make-up. Looks about twenty-five,

but has prematurely grey hair, and am conscious
that this gives me distinct satisfaction.

(Not very commendable reaction.)

Am overcome with astonishment when she
enquires of Commandant in brusque, official
tones: Isn't it time you had some lunch, darling?

Commandant for the first time raises her eyes
and answers No, darling, she can't possibly
bother with lunch, but she wants a staff car instantly, to go out to Wimbledon for her. It's
urgent.

Serena looks hopeful but remains modestly
silent while Commandant and Darling rustle
through quantities of lists and swear vigorously,
saying that it's a most extraordinary thing, the
Time-Sheets ought to be always available at a
second's notice, and they never *are*.

Darling eventually turns to Serena, just as
previous—and infinitely preferable—Messenger returns breathless, and asks curtly, Who
is on the Staff Car? Serena indicates that she is
herself scheduled for it, is asked why she didn't
say so, and commanded to get car out instantly
and dash to Wimbledon.

Am deeply impressed by this call to action, but disappointed when Commandant instructs her to go *straight* to No. 478 Mottisfont Road, Wimbledon, and ask for clean handkerchief, which Commandant forgot to bring this morning.

She is to come *straight* back, as quickly as possible, *with* the handkerchief. Has she, adds Commandant suspiciously, quite understood?

Serena replies that she has. Tell myself that in her place I should reply No, it's all too complicated for me to grasp—but judging from life-long experience, this is a complete fallacy and should in reality say nothing of the kind but merely wish, long afterwards, that I had.

Departure of Serena, in search, no doubt, of tin helmet and gas-mask, and am left, together with elderly Messenger, to be ignored by Commandant whilst she and Darling embark on earnest argument concerning Commandant's next meal, which turns out to be lunch, although time now five o'clock in the afternoon.

She must, says Darling, absolutely *must* have something. She has been here since nine o'clock and during that time what has she had? One cup of coffee and a tomato. It isn't enough on which to do a heavy day's work.

Commandant—writing again resumed and eyes again on paper—asserts that it's all she wants. She hasn't time for more. Does Darling realise that there's a *war* on, and not a minute to spare?

Yes, argues Darling, but she could eat something without leaving her desk for a second. Will she try some soup?

No.

Then a cup of tea and some buns?

No, no, no. *Nothing.*

She *must* take some black coffee. Absolutely and definitely must. Oh, very well, cries Commandant—at the same time striking table quite violently with her hand, which produces confusion among the papers. (Can foresee fresh trouble with mislaid Time-Sheets in immediate future.) Very well—black coffee, and she'll have it here. Instantly.

Darling dashes from the room throwing murderous look at elderly Messenger who has temporarily obstructed the dash.

Commandant writes more frenziedly than ever and snaps out single word *What*, which sounds like a bark, and is evidently addressed to Messenger, who respectfully lays Canteen Time-Sheet on table. This not a success, as Commandant snatches it up again and cries *Not* on the table, my God, *not* on the table! and scans it at red-hot speed.

She then writes again, as though nothing had happened.

Decide that if I am to be here indefinitely I may as well sit down, and do so.

Elderly Messenger gives me terrified, but I think admiring, look. Evidently this display of initiative quite unusual, and am, in fact, rather struck by it myself.

Darling reappears with a tray. Black coffee has materialised and is flanked by large plate of scrambled eggs on toast, two rock-buns and a banana.

All are placed at Commandant's elbow and she wields a fork with one hand and continues to write with the other.

Have sudden impulse to quote to her historical anecdote of British Sovereign remarking to celebrated historian: Scribble, scribble, scribble, Mr. Gibbon.

Do not, naturally, give way to it.

Darling asks me coldly If I want anything, and on my replying that I have offered my services to Canteen tells me to go *at once* to Mrs. Peacock. Decide to assume that this means I am to be permitted to serve my country, if only with coffee and eggs, so depart, and Elderly Messenger creeps out with me.

I ask if she will be kind enough to take me to Mrs. Peacock and she says Of course, and we proceed quietly—no rushing or dashing. (*Query:* Will not this dilatory spirit lose us the war? *Answer:* Undoubtedly, Nonsense!) Make note not to let myself be affected by aura of agitation surrounding Commandant and friend.

Messenger takes me past cars, ambulances, Rest-room, from which unholy din of feminine voices proceeds, and gives me information.

A Society Deb. is working in the Canteen. She is the only one in the whole place. A reporter came to interview her once and she was photographed kneeling on one knee beside an

[99]

ambulance wheel, holding tools and things. Photograph published in several papers and underneath it was printed: Debutante Jennifer Jamfather Stands By on Home Front.

Reach Mrs. Peacock, who is behind Canteen counter, sitting on a box, and looks kind but harassed.

She has a bad leg. Not a permanent bad leg but it gets in her way, and she will be glad of extra help.

Feel much encouraged by this. Nobody else has made faintest suggestion of being glad of extra help—on the contrary.

Raise my voice so as to be audible above gramophone ("Little Sir Echo") and wireless (. . . And so, bairns, we bid Goodbye to Bonnie Scotland)—roarings and bellowings of Darts Finals being played in a corner, and clatter of dishes from the kitchen—and announce that I am Come to Help—which I think sounds as if I were one of the Ministering Children Forty Years After.

Mrs. Peacock, evidently too dejected even to summon up customary formula that there is nothing for me to do except Stand By as she is turning helpers away by the hundred every hour, smiles rather wanly and says I am very kind.

What, I enquire, can I do?

At the moment, nothing. (Can this be a recrudescence of Stand By theme?)

The five o'clock rush is over, and the seven o'clock rush hasn't begun. Mrs. Peacock is taking the opportunity of sitting for a moment. She heroically makes rather half-hearted attempt at offering me half packing-case, which I at once decline and ask about her leg.

Mrs. P. displays it, swathed in bandages beneath her stocking, and tells me how her husband had two boxes of sand, shovel and bucket prepared for emergency use——(this evidently euphemism for incendiary bombs) and gave full instructions to household as to use of them, demonstrating in back garden. Mrs. P. herself took part in this, she adds impressively. I say Yes, yes, to encourage her, and she goes on. Telephone call then obliged her to leave the scene——interpolation here about nature of the call involving explanation as to young married niece——husband a sailor, dear little baby with beautiful big blue eyes——from whom call emanated.

Ninth pip-pip-pip compelled Mrs. P. to ring off and, on retracing her steps, she crossed first floor landing on which husband, without a word of warning, had meanwhile caused box of sand, shovel and bucket to be ranged, with a view to permanent instalment there. Mrs. P.—not expecting any of them—unfortunately caught her foot in the shovel, crashed into the sand-boxes, and was cut to the bone by edge of the bucket.

She concludes by telling me that it really was a lesson. Am not clear of what nature, or to whom, but sympathise very much and say I shall hope to save her as much as possible.

Hope this proceeds from unmixed benevolence, but am inclined to think it is largely actuated by desire to establish myself definitely as canteen worker—in which it meets with success.

Return to Buckingham Street flat again coincides with exit of owner, who at once enquires whether I have ascertained whereabouts of nearest air-raid shelter.

Well, yes, I have in a way. That is to say, the A.R.P.[1] establishment in Adelphi is within three minutes' walk, and I could go there.

[1] Air Raid Precautions.

Owner returns severely that that is Not Good Enough. He must beg of me to take this question seriously, and pace the distance between bedroom and shelter and find out how long it would take to get there in the event of an emergency. Moreover, he declares there is a shelter nearer than the Adelphi, and proceeds to indicate it.

Undertake, reluctantly, to conduct a brief rehearsal of my own exodus under stimulus of air-raid alarm, and subsequently do so.

This takes the form of rather interesting little experiment in which I lay out warm clothes, heavy coat, *Our Mutual Friend*—Shakespeare much more impressive but cannot rise to it— small bottle of boiled sweets—sugar said to increase energy and restore impaired morale— and electric torch. Undress and get into bed, then sound imaginary tocsin, look at my watch, and leap up.

Dressing is accomplished without mishap and proceed downstairs and into street with *Our Mutual Friend*, boiled sweets and electric torch. Am shocked to find myself strongly inclined to run like a lamplighter, in spite of repeated in-

structions issued to the contrary. If this is the
case when no raid at all is taking place, ask myself what it would be like with bombers overhead—and do not care to contemplate reply.

Street seems very dark, and am twice in col-
lision with other pedestrians. Reaction to this
is merry laughter on both sides. (Effect of
black-out on national hilarity quite excellent.)

Turn briskly down side street and up to entrance of air-raid shelter, which turns out to be
locked. Masculine voice enquires where I think
I am going, and I say, Is it the police? No, it is
the Air-raid Warden. Explain entire situation;
he commends my forethought and says that on
the first sound of siren alarm He Will be There.
Assure him in return that in that case we shall
meet, as I shall also Be There, with equal celerity, and we part—cannot say whether temporarily or for ever.

Wrist-watch, in pocket of coat, reveals that
entire performance has occupied four and a half
minutes only.

Am much impressed, and walk back reflecting on my own efficiency and wondering how
best to ensure that it shall be appreciated by

Robert, to whom I propose to write spirited account.

Return to flat reveals that I have left all the electric lights burning—though behind blue shades—and forgotten gas-mask, still lying in readiness on table.

Decide to put off writing account to Robert.

Undress and get into bed again, leaving clothes and other properties, ready as before—gas-mask in prominent position on shoes—but realise that if I have to go through whole performance all over again to-night, shall be very angry indeed.

October 2nd.—No alarm takes place. Wake at two o'clock and hear something which I think may be a warbling note from a siren—which we have been told to expect—but if so, warbler very poor and indeterminate performer, and come to the conclusion that it is not worth my attention and go to sleep again.

Post—now very late every day—does not arrive until after breakfast.

Short note from Robert informs me that all is well, he does not care about the way the Russians are behaving—(he never has)—his

A.R.P.[1] office has more volunteers than he knows what to do with—and young Cramp from the garage, who offered to learn method of dealing with unexploded bombs, has withdrawn after ten minutes' instruction on the grounds that he thinks it seems rather dangerous.

Robert hopes I am enjoying the black-out— which I think is satirical—and has not forwarded joint letter received from Robin as there is nothing much in it. (Could willingly strangle him for this.)

Vicky's letter, addressed to me, makes some amends, as she writes ecstatically about heavenly new dormitory, divine concert and utterly twee air-raid shelter newly constructed (towards which parents will no doubt be asked to contribute). Vicky's only complaint is to the effect that no air-raid has yet occurred, which is very dull.

Also receive immensely long and chatty letter from Aunt Blanche. Marigold and Margery are well, Doreen Fitzgerald and Cook have failed to reach identity of views regarding ques-

[1] Air Raid Precautions.

tion of the children's supper but this has now been adjusted by Aunt Blanche and I am not to worry, and Robert seems quite all right, though not saying much.

Our Vicar's Wife has been to tea—worn to a thread and looking like death—but has declared that she is getting on splendidly and the evacuees are settling down, and a nephew of a friend of hers, in the Militia, has told his mother, who has written it to his aunt, who has passed it on to Our Vicar's Wife, that all Berlin is seething with discontent, and a revolution in Germany is scheduled for the first Monday in November.

Is this, asks Aunt Blanche rhetorically, what the Press calls Wishful Thinking?

She concludes with affectionate enquiries as to my well-being, begs me to go and see old Uncle A. when I have time, and is longing to hear what post I have been offered by the Ministry of Information. *P.S.:* What about the Sweep? Cook has been asking.

Have never yet either left home, or got back to it, without being told that Cook is asking about the Sweep.

Large proportion of mail consists of letters, full of eloquence, from trades people who say that they are now faced with a difficult situation which will, however, be improved on receipt of my esteemed cheque.

Irresistible conviction comes over me that my situation is even more difficult than theirs, and, moreover, no cheques are in the least likely to come and improve it.

Turn, in hopes of consolation, to remainder of mail and am confronted with Felicity Fairmead's writing—very spidery—on envelope, and typewritten letter within, which she has forgotten to sign. Tells me that she is using typewriter with a view to training for war work, and adds candidly that she can't help hoping war may be over before she finds it. This, says Felicity, is awful, she knows very well, but she can't help it. She is deeply ashamed of her utter uselessness, as she is doing nothing whatever except staying as Paying Guest in the country with delicate friend whose husband is in France, and who has three small children, also delicate, and one maid who isn't any use, so that Felicity and friend make the beds, look after the children, do most of the cooking and keep the garden in order. Both feel how wrong it is not to be doing real work for the country, and this has driven Felicity to the typewriter and friend to the knitting of socks and Balaclava helmets.

Felicity concludes with wistful supposition that *I* am doing something splendid.

Should be very sorry to enlighten her on this point, and shall feel constrained to leave letter unanswered until reality of my position corresponds rather more to Felicity's ideas.

Meanwhile, have serious thoughts of sending copies of her letter to numerous domestic helpers of my acquaintance who have seen fit to leave their posts at a moment's notice in order to seek more spectacular jobs elsewhere.

Remaining item in the post is letter-card—which I have customary difficulty in tearing open and only succeed at the expense of one corner—and proves to be from Barbara Carruthers *née* Blenkinsop, now living in Midlands. She informs me that this war is upsetting her very much: it really is dreadful for *her*, she says, because she has children, and situation may get very difficult later on and they may

have to do without things and she has always
taken so much trouble to see that they have
everything. They are at present in Westmor-
land, but this is a considerable expense and
moreover petrol regulations make it impossible
to go and see them, and train-service—about
which Barbara is indignant and says it is *very*
hard on her—most unsatisfactory. How long
do I think war is going on? She had arranged
for her elder boys to go to excellent Preparatory
School near London this autumn, but school has
moved to Wales, which isn't at all the same
thing and Barbara does feel it's rather too bad.
And what do I think about food shortage? It is
most unfair if her children are to be rationed,
and she would even be prepared to pay extra for
them to have additional supplies. She concludes
by sending me her love and enquiring casually
whether Robin has been sent to France yet, or is
he just too young?

Am so disgusted at Barbara's whole attitude
that I dramatically tear up letter into fragments
and cast it from me, but realise later that it
should have been kept, in order that I might
send suitable reply.

Draft this in my own mind several times in course of the day, until positively vitriolic indictment is evolved which will undoubtedly never see the light of day, and would probably land me in the Old Bailey on a charge of defamatory libel if it did.

Purchase overall for use in Canteen, debate the question of trousers and decide that I must be strong-minded enough to remain in customary clothing which is perfectly adequate to work behind the counter. Find myself almost immediately afterwards trying on very nice pair of navy-blue slacks, thinking that I look well in them and buying them.

Am prepared to take any bet that I shall wear them every time I go on duty.

As this is not to happen till nine o'clock to-night, determine to look up the Weatherbys, who might possibly be able to suggest whole-time National Service job—and old Uncle A. about whom Aunt Blanche evidently feels anxious.

Ring up Uncle A.—his housekeeper says he will be delighted to see me at tea-time—and also Mrs. Weatherby, living in Chelsea, who in-

vites me to lunch and says her husband, distinguished Civil Servant, will be in and would much like to meet me. Imagination instantly suggests that he has heard of me (in what connection, cannot possibly conceive), and, on learning that he is to be privileged to see me at his table, will at once realise that Civil Service would be the better for my assistance in some highly authoritative capacity.

Spend hours wondering what clothes would make me look most efficient, but am quite clear *not* slacks for the Civil Service. Finally decide on black coat and skirt, white blouse with frill of austere, *not* frilly, type, and cone-shaped black hat. Find that I look like inferior witch in third-rate pantomime in the latter, and take it off again. Only alternative is powder-blue with rainbow-like swathings, quite out of the question. Feel myself obliged to go out and buy small black hat, with brim like a jockey-cap and red edging. Have no idea whether this is in accordance with Civil Service tastes or not, but feel that I look nice in it.

Walk to Chelsea, and on looking into small mirror in handbag realise that I don't, after all. Can do nothing about it, and simply ask hall porter for Mrs. Weatherby, and am taken up in lift to sixth-floor flat, very modern and austere, colouring entirely neutral, and statuette —to me wholly revolting—of misshapen green cat occupying top of bookcase, dominating whole of the room.

Hostess comes in—cannot remember if we are on Christian-name terms or not, but inclined to think not and do not risk it—greets me very kindly and again repeats that her husband wishes to meet me.

(Civil Service appointment definitely in sight, and decide to offer Serena job as my private secretary.)

Discuss view of the river from window—Mrs. Weatherby says block of flats would be an excellent target from the air, at which we both laugh agreeably—extraordinary behaviour of the Ministry of Information, and delightful autumnal colouring in neighbourhood of Bovey Tracy, which Mrs. Weatherby says she knows well.

Entrance of Mr. Weatherby puts an end to this interchange, and we are introduced. Mr. W. very tall and cadaverous, and has a beard, which makes me think of Agrippa.

He says that he has been wishing to meet me,

but does not add why. Produces sherry and we talk about black-out, President Roosevelt—I say that his behaviour throughout entire crisis has been magnificent and moves me beyond measure—Mrs. Weatherby agrees, but Agrippa seems surprised and I feel would like to contradict me but politeness forbids—and we pass on to cocker spaniels, do not know how or why.

Admirable parlourmaid—uniform, demeanour and manner all equally superior to those of Winnie, or even departed May—announces that Luncheon is served, madam, and just as I prepare to swallow remainder of sherry rapidly, pallid elderly gentleman crawls in, leaning on stick and awakening in me instant conviction that he is not long for this world.

Impression turns out to be not without foundation as it transpires that he is Agrippa's uncle, and has recently undergone major operation at London Nursing Home but was desired to leave it at five minutes' notice in order that bed should be available if and when required. Uncle asserts that he met this—as well he might—with protests but was unfortunately too feeble to enforce them and accordingly found himself, so he declares, on the pavement while still unable to stand. From this fearful plight he has been retrieved by Agrippa, and given hospitality of which he cannot speak gratefully enough.

Story concludes with examples of other, similar cases, of which we all seem to know several, and Mrs. Weatherby's solemn assurance that all the beds of all the Hospitals and Nursing Homes in England are standing empty, and that no civilian person is to be allowed to be ill until the war is over.

Agrippa's uncle shakes his head, and looks worse than ever, and soon after he has pecked at chicken soufflé, waved away sweet omelette and turned his head from the sight of Camembert cheese, he is compelled by united efforts of the Weatherbys to drink a glass of excellent port and retire from the room.

They tell me how very ill he has been—can well believe it—and that there was another patient even more ill, in room next to his at Nursing Home, who was likewise desired to leave. She, however, defeated the authorities by dying before they had time to get her packing done.

Find myself exclaiming "Well done!" in enthusiastic tone before I have time to stop myself, and am shocked. So, I think, are the Weatherbys—rightly.

Agrippa changes the conversation and asks my opinion about the value of the natural resources of Moravia. Fortunately answers his own question, at considerable length.

Cannot see that any of this, however interesting, is leading in the direction of war work for me.

On returning to drawing-room and superb coffee which recalls Cook's efforts at home rather sadly to my mind—I myself turn conversation forcibly into desired channel.

What an extraordinary thing it is, I say, that so many intelligent and experienced people are not, so far as one can tell, being utilised by the Government in any way!

Mrs. Weatherby replies that she thinks most people who are *really* trained for anything worth while have found no difficulty whatever in getting jobs, and Agrippa declares that it is largely a question of Standing By, and will continue to be so for many months to come.

Does he, then, think that this will be a long war?

Agrippa, assuming expression of preternatural discretion, replies that he must not, naturally, commit himself. Government officials, nowadays, have to be exceedingly careful in what they say as I shall, he has no doubt, readily understand.

Mrs. Weatherby strikes in to the effect that it is difficult to see how the war can be a very *short* one, and yet it seems unlikely to be a very *long* one.

I enquire whether she thinks it is going to be a middling one, and then feel I have spoken flippantly and that both disapprove of me.

Should like to leave at once, but custom and decency alike forbid as have only this moment finished coffee.

Ask whether anything has been heard of Pamela Pringle, known to all three of us, at which Agrippa's face lights up in the most extraordinary way and he exclaims that she is, poor dear, quite an invalid but as charming as ever.

Mrs. Weatherby—face not lighting up at all but, on the contrary resembling a thunder-cloud —explains that Pamela, since war started, has developed unspecified form of Heart and retired to large house near the New Forest where she lies on the sofa, in *eau-de-nil* velvet wrapper, and has all her friends down to stay in turns.

Her husband has a job with the Army and is said to be in Morocco, and she has despatched the children to relations in America, saying that this is a terrible sacrifice, but done for their own sakes.

Can only reply, although I hope indulgently that it all sounds to me exactly like dear Pamela. This comment more of a success with Mrs. W. than with Agrippa, who stands up—looks as if he might touch the ceiling—and says that he must get back to work.

Have abandoned all serious hope of his offering me a post of national importance, or even of no importance at all, but put out timid feeler to the effect that he must be very busy just now.

Yes, yes, he is. He won't get back before eight o'clock to-night, if then. At one time it was eleven o'clock, but things are for the moment a little easier, though no doubt this is only temporary. (*Query:* Why is it that all those occupied in serving the country are completely overwhelmed by pressure of work but do not

apparently dream of utilising assistance pressed
upon them by hundreds of willing helpers? *Answer* comes there none.)

Agrippa and I exchange unenthusiastic farewells, but he sticks to his guns to the last and
says that he has always wanted to meet me.
Does not, naturally, add whether the achievement of this ambition has proved disappointing
or the reverse.

Linger on for a few moments in frail and un-
worthy hope that Mrs. Weatherby may say
something more, preferably scandalous, about
Pamela Pringle, but she only refers, rather
bleakly, to Agrippa's uncle and his low state of
health and asserts that she does not know what
the British Medical Association can be thinking about.

Agree that I don't either—which is true not
only now but at all times—and take my leave.
Tell her how much I have liked seeing them
both, and am conscious of departing from spirit
of truth in saying so, but cannot, obviously, inform her that the only parts of the entertainment I have really enjoyed are her excellent
lunch and hearing about Pamela.

Go out in search of bus—all very few and

far between now—and contemplate visit to hairdresser's, but conscience officiously points out that visits to hairdresser constitute an unnecessary expense and could very well be replaced by ordinary shampoo in bedroom basin at flat. Inner prompting—probably the Devil—urges that Trade must be Kept Going and that it is my duty to help on the commercial life of the nation.

Debate this earnestly, find that bus has passed the spot at which I intended to get out, make undecided effort to stop it, then change my mind and sit down again and am urged by conductor to Make up My Mind. I shall have to move a lot faster than that, he jocosely remarks, when them aeroplanes are overhead. Much amusement is occasioned to passengers in general, and we all part in high spirits.

Am much too early for Uncle A. and walk about the streets—admire balloons which look perfectly entrancing—think about income-tax, so rightly described as crushing, and decide not to be crushed at all but readjust ideas about what constitutes reasonable standard of living, and learn to cook for self and family—and look at innumerable posters announcing contents of evening papers.

Lowest level seems to me to be reached by one which features *exposé*, doubtless apocryphal, of Hitler's sex life—but am not pleased with another which enquires—idiotically— Why Not Send Eden to Russia?

Could suggest hundreds of reasons why not, and none in favour.

Remaining posters all display ingenious statements, implying that tremendous advance has been made somewhere by Allies, none of whom have suffered any casualties at all, with enormous losses to enemy.

Evolve magnificent piece of rhetoric, designed to make clear once and for all what does, and what does not, constitute good propaganda, and this takes me to Mansions in Kensington at the very top of which dwell Uncle A. and housekeeper, whose peculiar name is Mrs. Mouse.

Sensation quite distinctly resembling small trickle of ice-cold water running down spine assails me, at the thought that rhetoric on propaganda will all be wasted, since no Government Department wishes for my assistance—but must banish this discouraging reflection and remind myself that at least I am to be allowed a few hours' work in Canteen.

Hall porter—old friend—is unfortunately inspired to greet me with expressions of surprise and disappointment that I am not in uniform. Most ladies are, nowadays, he says. His circle of acquaintances evidently more fortunate than mine. Reply that I have been trying to join something—but can see he doesn't believe it.

We go up very slowly and jerkily in aged Victorian lift—pitch dark and smells of horsehair—and porter informs me that nearly all the flats are empty, but he doubts whether 'Itler himself could move the old gentleman. Adds conversationally that, in his view, it is a *funny* war. Very funny indeed. He supposes we might say that it hasn't hardly begun yet, has it? Agree, though reluctantly, that we might.

Still, says the hall porter as lift comes to an abrupt stop, we couldn't very well have allowed '*im* to carry on as he was doing, could we, and will I please mind the step.

I do mind the step—which is about three

feet higher than the landing—and ring Uncle
A.'s bell.

Can distinctly see Mrs. Mouse applying one
eye to ground-glass panel at top of door before
she opens it and welcomes my arrival. In reply
to enquiry she tells me that Uncle A. is remark-
ably well and has been all along, and that you'd
never give him seventy, let alone eighty-one.
She adds philosophically that nothing isn't
going to make him stir and she supposes, with
hearty laughter, that he'll never be satisfied
until he's had the both of them smothered in
poison gas, set fire to, blown sky-high and buried
under the whole of the buildings.

Point out that this is surely excessive and
enquire whether they have a shelter in the basement. Oh yes, replies Mrs. M., but she had the
work of the world to get him down there when
the early-morning alarm was given, at the very
beginning of the war, as he refused to move
until fully dressed and with his teeth in. The
only thing that has disturbed him at all, she
adds, is the thought that he is taking no active
part in the war.

She then conducts me down familiar narrow

passage carpeted in red, with chocolate-and-gilt wallpaper, and into rather musty but agreeable drawing-room crammed with large pieces of furniture, potted palm, family portraits in gilt frames, glass-fronted cupboards, china, books, hundreds of newspapers and old copies of *Blackwood's Magazine*, and grand piano on which nobody has played for about twenty-seven years.

Uncle A. rises alertly from mahogany knee-hole writing-table—very upright and distinguished-looking typical Diplomatic Service—(quite misleading, Uncle A. retired stockbroker)—and receives me most affectionately.

He tells me that I look tired—so I probably do, compared with Uncle A. himself—commands Mrs. M. to bring tea, and wheels up an armchair for me in front of magnificent old-fashioned coal fire. Can only accept it gratefully and gaze in admiration at Uncle A.'s slim figure, abundant white hair and general appearance of jauntiness.

He enquires after Robert, the children and his sister—whom he refers to as poor dear old Blanche—(about fifteen years his junior)—and tells me that he has offered his services to the War Office and has had a very civil letter in acknowledgment, but they have not, as yet, actually found a niche for him. No doubt, however, of their doing so in time.

The Government is, in Uncle A.'s opinion, underrating the German strength, and as he himself knew Germany well in his student days at Heidelberg, he is writing a letter to *The Times* in order to make the position better understood.

He asks about evacuees—has heard all about them from Blanche—and tells me about his great-niece in Shropshire. She is sitting in her manor-house waiting for seven evacuated children whom she has been told to expect; beds are already made, everything waiting, but children haven't turned up. I suggest that this is reminiscent of Snow White and seven little dwarfs, only no little dwarfs.

Uncle A. appears to be immeasurably amused and repeats at intervals: Snow White and no little dwarfs. Capital, capital!

Tea is brought in by Mrs. M., and Uncle A. declines my offer of pouring out and does it him-

self, and plies me with hot scones, apricot jam and home-made gingerbread. All is the work of Mrs. M. and I tell Uncle A. that she is a treasure, at which he looks rather surprised and says she's a good gel enough and does what she's told.

Can only remember, in awe-stricken silence, that Mrs. M. has been in Uncle A.'s service for the past forty-six years.

Take my leave very soon afterwards and make a point of stating that I have presently to go on duty at A.R.P.[1] Canteen, to which Uncle A. replies solicitously that I mustn't go overdoing it.

He then escorts me to the lift, commands the hall porter to look after me and call a cab should I require one, and remains waving a hand while lift, in a series of irregular leaps, bears me downstairs.

No cab is required—hall porter does not so much as refer to it—and take a bus back to the Strand.

Bathroom has now familiar notice pinned on door—"Occupied"—which I assume to be Se-

[1] Air Raid Precautions.

rena, especially on finding large bunch of pink gladioli in sitting-room, one empty sherry-glass, and several biscuit crumbs on rug. Moreover, black-out has been achieved and customary sheets of paper pinned up, and also customary number of drawing-pins strewn over the floor.

Serena emerges from bathroom, very pink, and says she hopes it's All Right, and I say it is, and thank her for gladioli, to which she replies candidly that flowers are so cheap nowadays they're being practically *given* away.

She asks what I have been doing, and I relate my experiences—Serena carries sympathy so far as to declare that Mr. Weatherby ought to be taken out and shot and that Mrs. W. doesn't sound much of a one either, but Uncle A. too adorable for words.

She then reveals that she came round on purpose to suggest we should have supper at Canteen together before going on duty.

Am delighted to agree, and change into trousers and overall. Greatly relieved when Serena ecstatically admires both.

Extraordinary thought that she is still only known to me as Serena Fiddlededee.

1.30 A.M.—Return from Canteen after evening of activity which has given me agreeable illusion that I am now wholly indispensable to the Allies in the conduct of the war.

Canteen responsibilities, so far as I am concerned, involve much skipping about with orders, memorising prices of different brands of cigarettes—which mostly have tiresome halfpenny tacked on to round sum, making calculation difficult—and fetching of fried eggs, rashers, sausages-and-mashed and Welsh rarebits from kitchen.

Mrs. Peacock—leg still giving trouble—very kind, and fellow workers pleasant; old Mrs. Winter-Gammon only to be seen in the distance, and Serena not at all.

Am much struck by continuous pandemonium of noise in Canteen, but become more accustomed to it every moment, and feel that air-raid warning, by comparison, would pass over my head quite unnoticed.

October 3rd.—Old Mrs. Winter-Gammon develops tendency, rapidly becoming fixed habit, of propping herself against Canteen counter, smoking cigarettes and chattering merrily. She

asserts that she can do without sleep, without rest, without food and without fresh air. Am reluctantly forced to the conclusion that she can.

Conversation of Mrs. W.-G. is wholly addressed to me, since Mrs. Peacock—leg in no way improved—remains glued to her box from which she can manipulate Cash-register—and leave Debutante to do one end of the counter, Colonial young creature with blue eyes in the middle, and myself at the other end.

Custom goes entirely to Debutante, who is prettyish, and talks out of one corner of tightly-shut mouth in quite unintelligible mutter, and Colonial, who is amusing. Am consequently left to company of Granny Bo-Peep.

She says roguishly that we old ones must be content to put up with one another and before I have time to think out civil formula in which to tell her that I disagree, goes on to add that, really, it's quite ridiculous the way all the boys come flocking round her. They like, she thinks, being mothered—and yet, at the same time, she somehow finds she can keep them laughing. It isn't that she's specially witty, whatever some of her clever men friends—such as W. B. Yeats, Rudyard Kipling and Lord Oxford and Asquith —may have said in the past. It's just that she was born, she supposes, under a dancing star. Like Beatrice.

(If Granny Bo-Peep thinks that I am going to ask her who Beatrice was, she is under a mistake. Would willingly submit to torture rather than do so, even if I didn't know, which I do.)

She has the audacity to ask, after suitable pause, if I know my Shakespeare.

Reply No not particularly, very curtly, and take an order for two Welsh rarebits and one Bacon-and-sausage to the kitchen. Have barely returned before Granny Bo-Peep is informing me that her quotation was from that lovely comedy *Much Ado About Nothing*. Do I know *Much Ado About Nothing?*

Yes, I do—and take another order for Sausages-and-mashed. Recollection comes before me, quite unnecessarily, of slight confusion which has always been liable to occur in my mind, as to which of Shakespeare's comedies is called *As You Like It* and which *Much Ado*

[130]

About Nothing. Should be delighted to tell old Mrs. W.-G. that she has made a mistake, but am not sufficiently positive myself.

Moreover, she gives me no opportunity.

Have I heard, she wants to know, from poor Blanche? I ask Why poor? and try to smile pleasantly so as to show that I am not being disagreeable—which I am. Well, says Granny Bo-Peep indulgently, she always thinks that poor Blanche—perfect dear though she is—is a wee bit lacking in *fun*. Granny Bo-Peep herself has such a keen sense of the ridiculous that it has enabled her to bear all her troubles where others, less fortunately endowed, would almost certainly have gone to pieces. Many, many years ago her doctor—one of the best-known men in Harley Street—said to her: Mrs. Winter-Gammon, by rights you ought not to be alive to-day. You ought to be dead. Your health, your sorrows, your life of hard work for others, all should have killed you long, long ago. What has kept you alive? Nothing but your wonderful spirits.

And I am not, says Mrs. W.-G., to think for one instant that she is telling me this in a boast-

[131]

ful spirit. Far from it. Her vitality, her gaiety, her youthfulness and her great sense of humour have all been bestowed upon her from Above. She has had nothing to do but rejoice in the possession of these attributes and do her best to make others rejoice in them too.

Could well reply to this that if she has succeeded with others no better than she has with me, all has been wasted—but do not do so.

Shortly afterwards Commandant comes in, at which Mrs. Peacock rises from her box, blue-eyed young Colonial drops a Beans-on-Toast on the floor, and Society Deb. pays no attention whatever.

Granny Bo-Peep nods at me very brightly, lights her fourteenth cigarette and retires to trestle-table on which she perches swinging her legs, and is instantly surrounded—to my fury—by crowd of men, all obviously delighted with her company.

Commandant asks what we have for supper—averting eyes from me as she speaks—and on being handed list goes through items in tones of utmost contempt.

She then orders two tomatoes on toast. Friend

—known to me only as Darling—materialises behind her, and cries out that Surely, surely, darling, she's going to have more than *that*. She must. She isn't going to be allowed to make her supper on tomatoes—it isn't *enough*.

Commandant makes slight snarling sound, but no other answer, and I retire to kitchen with order, leaving Darling still expostulating.

Previously ordered Sausages-and-mashed, Welsh rarebit, Bacon-and-sausage are now ready, and I distribute them, nearly falling over distressed young Colonial who is scraping up baked beans off the floor. She asks madly what she is to do with them and I reply briefly: Dustbin.

Commandant asks me sharply where her tomatoes are and I reply, I hope equally sharply, In the frying-pan. She instantly takes the wind out of my sails by replying that she didn't say she wanted them fried. She wants the *bread* fried, and the tomatoes uncooked. Darling breaks out into fresh objections and I revise order given to kitchen.

Cook is not pleased.

Previous orders now paid for over counter,

[133]

and Mrs. Peacock, who has conducted cash transactions with perfect accuracy hitherto, asserts that ninepence from half a crown leaves one and sixpence change. Ambulance driver to whom she hands this sum naturally demands an explanation, and the whole affair comes to the notice of the Commandant, who addresses a withering rebuke to poor Mrs. P. Am very sorry for her indeed and should like to help her if I could, but this a vain aspiration at the moment and can only seek to distract attention of Commandant by thrusting at her plate of fried bread and un-fried tomatoes. She takes no notice whatever and finishes what she has to say, and Darling makes imperative signs to me that I am guilty of *lèse-majesté* in interrupting. Compose short but very pungent little essay on Women in Authority. (*Query:* Could not leaflets be dropped by our own Air Force, in their spare moments, on Women's Organisations all over the British Isles?)

Sound like a sharp bark recalls me, and is nothing less than Commandant asking if *that* is her supper.

Yes, it is.

Then will I take it back at once and have it put into the oven. It's stone cold.

Debate flinging the whole thing at her head, which I should enjoy doing, but instincts of civilisation unfortunately prevail and I decide —probable rationalising process here—that it will impress her more to display perfect good-breeding.

Accordingly reply Certainly in tones of icy composure—but am not sure they don't sound as though I were consciously trying to be refined, and wish I'd let it alone. Moreover Commandant, obviously not in the least ashamed of herself, merely tells me to be quick about it, please, in insufferably authoritative manner.

Cook angrier than ever.

Very pretty girl with curls all over her head and waist measurement apparently eighteen-inch, comes and leans up against the counter and asks me to advise her in choice between Milk Chocolate Bar and Plain Chocolate Biscuit.

Deb. addresses something to her which sounds like Hay-o Mule! and which I realise, minutes later, may have been Hallo, Muriel. Am much flattered when Muriel merely shakes her curls in reply and continues to talk to me. Am unfortunately compelled to leave her, still undecided, in order to collect Commandant's supper once more.

Cook hands it to me with curtly expressed, but evidently heartfelt, hope that it may choke her. Pretend I haven't heard, but find myself exchanging very eloquent look with Cook all the same.

Plate, I am glad to say unpleasantly hot, is snatched from me by Darling and passed on to Commandant, who in her turn snatches it and goes off without so much as a Thank you.

Rumour spreads all round the underworld—cannot say why or from where—that the German bombers are going to raid London to-night. They are, it is said, *expected*. Think this sounds very odd, and quite as though we had invited them. Nobody seems seriously depressed, and Society Deb. is more nearly enthusiastic than I have ever heard her and remarks Ra way baw way, out of one corner of her mouth. Cannot interpret this, and make very little attempt to do so. Have probably not missed much.

Night wears on; Mrs. Peacock looks pale
green and evidently almost incapable of stirring
from packing-case at all, but leg is not this time
to blame, all is due to Commandant, and Mrs.
P.'s failure in assessing change correctly. Feel
very sorry for her indeed.

Customary pandemonium of noise fills the
Canteen: We Hang up our Washing on the
Siegfried Line and bellow aloud requests that
our friends should Wish us Luck when they
Wave us Goodbye: old Mrs. Winter-Gammon
sits surrounded by a crowd of ambulance men,
stretcher-bearers and demolition workers talk
far into the night, and sound of voices from
Women's Restroom goes on steadily and cease-
lessly.

I become involved with sandwich-cutting and
think I am doing well until austere woman who
came on duty at midnight confronts me with a
desiccated-looking slice of bread and asks coldly
If I cut that?

Yes, I did.

Do I realise that one of those long loaves
ought to cut up into thirty-two slices, and that,

at the rate I'm doing it, not more than twenty-four could possibly be achieved?

Can only apologise and undertake—rashly, as I subsequently discover—to do better in future.

A lull occurs between twelve and one, and Mrs. Peacock—greener than ever—asks Do I think I can manage, if she goes home now? Her leg is paining her. Assure her that I can, but austere woman intervenes and declares that both of us can go. *She* is here now, and will see to everything.

Take her at her word and depart with Mrs. P.

Street pitch-dark but very quiet, peaceful and refreshing after the underworld. Starlight night, and am meditating a reference to Mars—hope it *is* Mars—when Mrs. Peacock abruptly enquires if I can tell her a book to read. She has an idea—cannot say why, or whence derived—that I know something about books.

Find myself denying it as though confronted with highly scandalous accusation, and am further confounded by finding myself unable to think of any book whatever except *Grimm's Fairy Tales*, which is obviously absurd. What, I

[138]

enquire in order to gain time, does Mrs. Peacock like in the way of books?

In times such as these, she replies very apologetically indeed, she thinks a novel is practically the only thing. Not a detective novel, not a novel about politics, nor about the unemployed, nothing to do with sex, and above all not a novel about life under the Nazi régime in Germany.

Inspiration immediately descends upon me and I tell her without hesitation to read a delightful novel called *The Priory* by Dorothy Whipple, which answers all requirements, and has a happy ending into the bargain.

Mrs. Peacock says it seems too good to be true, and she can hardly believe that *any* modern novel is as nice as all that, but I assure her that it is and that it is many years since I have enjoyed anything so much.

Mrs. P. thanks me again and again, I offer to help her to find her bus in the Strand—leg evidently giving out altogether in a few minutes—beg her to take my arm, which she does, and I immediately lead her straight into a pile of sandbags.

Heroic pretence from Mrs. P. that she doesn't really mind—she likes it—if anything, the jar will have *improved* the state of her leg. Say Good-night to her before she can perjure herself any further and help her into bus which may or may not be the one she wants.

Return to Buckingham Street and find it is nearly two o'clock. Decide that I must get to bed quickly—but find myself instead mysteriously impelled to wash stockings, write to Vicky, tidy up writing-desk, and cut stems and change water of Serena's gladioli.

Finally retire to bed with *The Daisy Chain* wishing we were all back in the England of the 'fifties.

October 4th.—Serena tells me that Brigadier Pinflitton is very sorry, he doesn't think the War Office likely to require my services. But she is to tell me that, in time, *all* will find jobs.

If I hear this even once again, from any source whatever, I cannot answer for consequences.

Serena, who brings me this exhilarating message, asks me to walk round the Embankment Gardens with her, as she has got leave to come out for an hour's fresh air on the distinct understanding that in the event of an air-raid warning she instantly flies back to her post.

We admire the flowers, which are lovely, and are gratified by the arrival of a balloon in the middle of the gardens, with customary Man and Lorry attached.

Serena informs me that Hitler's peace proposals—referred to on posters as "peace offensive"—will be refused, and we both approve of this course and say that any other would be unthinkable and express our further conviction that Hitler is in fearful jam, and knows it, and is heading for a catastrophe. He will, predicts Serena, go right off his head before so very long.

Then we shall be left, I point out, with Goering, Ribbentrop and Hess.

Serena brushes them aside, asserting that Goering, though *bad*, is at least a soldier and knows the rules—more or less—that Ribbentrop will be assassinated quite soon—and that Hess is a man of straw.

Hope she knows what she is talking about.

We also discuss the underworld, and Serena

declares that Granny Bo-Peep has offered to get up a concert on the premises and sing at it herself. She does not see how this is to be prevented.

Tells me that girl with curls—Muriel—is rather sweet and owns a Chow puppy whose photograph she has shown Serena, and the Chow looks *exactly* like Muriel and has curls too.

The Commandant, thinks Serena, will—like Hitler—have a breakdown quite soon. She and Darling had a quarrel at six o'clock this morning because Darling brought her a plate of minced ham and the Commandant refused to touch it on the grounds of having No Time.

Darling reported to have left the premises in a black fury.

We then go back to flat and I offer Serena tea, which she accepts, and biscuits. Reflection occurs to me—promoted by contrast between Serena and the Commandant—that Golden Mean not yet achieved between refusal to touch food at all, and inability to refrain from practically unbroken succession of odd cups of tea, coffee, and biscuits all day and all night.

Just as I am preparing to expound this further, telephone bell rings. Call is from Lady Blowfield: If I am not *terribly* busy will I forgive short notice and lunch with her to-morrow to meet exceedingly interesting man—Russian by birth, married a Roumanian but this a failure and subsequently married a Frenchwoman, who has now divorced him. Speaks every language *well*, and is absolutely certain to have inside information about the European situation. Works as a free-lance journalist. Naturally accept with alacrity and express gratitude for this exceptional opportunity.

Am I, solicitously adds Lady Blowfield, keeping fairly well? Voice sounds so anxious that I don't care to say in return that I've never been better in my life, so reply Oh yes, I'm fairly all right, in tone which suggests that I haven't slept or eaten for a week— which isn't the case at all.

(*Note:* Adaptability to another's point of view is one thing, and rank deceit quite another. Should not care to say under which heading my present behaviour must be listed.)

Lady Blowfield says Ah! compassionately,

[143]

down the telephone, and I feel the least I can do is ask after her and Sir Archibald, although knowing beforehand that she will give no good account of either.

Archie, poor dear, is fearfully over-worked and she is very, very anxious about him, and wishes he would come into the country for a week-end, but this is impossible. He has begged her to go without him, but she has refused because she *knows* that if she once leaves London, there will be an air-raid and the whole transport system of the country will be disorganised, communications will be cut off everywhere, petrol will be unobtainable, and the Government—if still in existence at all—flung into utter disarray.

Can only feel that if all this is to be the direct result of Lady Blowfield's going into Surrey for a week-end she had undoubtedly better remain where she is.

She further tells me—I think—that Turkey's attitude is still in doubt and that neither she nor Archie care for the look of things in the Kremlin, but much is lost owing to impatient mutterings of Serena who urges me to

ring off, and says Surely that's *enough*, and
How much longer am I going on saying the
same things over and over again?

Thank Lady Blowfield about three more
times for the invitation, repeat that I shall
look forward to seeing her and meeting cosmopolitan friend—she reiterates all his qualifications as an authority on international politics, and conversation finally closes.

Apologise to Serena, who says It doesn't
matter a bit, only she particularly wants to
talk to me and hasn't much time. (Thought she
had been talking to me ever since she arrived,
but evidently mistaken.)

Do I remember, says Serena, meeting J. L.
at her flat?

Certainly. He said Plato provided him with
escape literature.

Serena exclaims in tones of horror that he
isn't *really* like that. He's quite nice. Not a
great sense of humour, perhaps, but a *kind* man,
and not in the least conceited.

Agree that this is all to the good.

Do I think it would be a good plan to marry
him?

[145]

Look at Serena in surprise. She is wearing expression of abject wretchedness and seems unable to meet my eye.

Reply, without much originality, that a good deal depends on what she herself feels about it.

Oh, says Serena, she doesn't know. She hasn't the slightest idea. That's why she wants my advice. Everyone seems to be getting married: haven't I noticed the announcements in *The Times* lately?

Yes, I have, and they have forcibly recalled 1914 and the three succeeding years to my mind. Reflections thus engendered have not been wholly encouraging. Still, the present question, I still feel, hinges on what Serena herself feels about J. L.

Serena says dispassionately that she likes him, she admires his work, she finds it very easy to get on with him, and she doesn't suppose they would make more of a hash of things than most people.

If that, I say, is all, better leave it alone.

Serena looks slightly relieved and thanks me.

I venture to ask her whether she has quite discounted the possibility of falling in love, and

Serena replies sadly that she has. She used to fall in love quite often when she was younger, but it always ended in disappointment, and anyway the *technique* of the whole thing has changed, and people never get married now just *because* they've fallen in love. It's an absolutely understood thing.

Then why, I ask, *do* they get married?

Mostly, replies Serena, because they want to make a change.

I assure her, with the greatest emphasis, that this is an inadequate reason for getting married. Serena is most grateful and affectionate, promises to do nothing in a hurry, and says that I have helped her enormously—which I know to be quite untrue.

Just as she is leaving, association of ideas with announcement in *The Times* leads me to admit that she is still only known to me as Serena Fiddlededee, owing to Aunt Blanche's extraordinary habit of always referring to her thus. Serena screams with laughter, asserts that nowadays one has to know a person *frightfully* well before learning their surname, and that hers is Brown with no E.

October 5th.—Lunch with Lady Blowfield and am privileged to meet cosmopolitan friend.

He turns out to be very wild-looking young man, hair all over the place and large eyes, and evidently unversed in uses of nail-brush. Has curious habit of speaking in two or three languages more or less at once, which is very impressive as he is evidently thoroughly at home in all—but cannot attempt to follow all he says.

Sir Archibald not present. He is, says Lady Blowfield, more occupied than ever owing to Hitler's iniquitous peace proposals. (Should like to ask what, exactly, he is doing about them, but difficult, if not impossible, to word this civilly.)

Young cosmopolitan—introduced as Monsieur Gitnik—asserts in French, that *Ce fou d'Itler fera un dernier attentat, mais, il n'y a que lui qui s'imagine que cela va réussir.* Reply *En effet*, in what I hope is excellent French, and Monsieur Gitnik turns to me instantly and makes me a long speech in what I think must be Russian.

Look him straight in the eye and say very

Mr. Gitnik.

rapidly *Da, da, da!* which is the only Russian word I know, and am shattered when he exclaims delightedly, Ah, you speak Russian?

Can only admit that I do not, and he looks disappointed and Lady Blowfield enquires whether he can tell us what is going to happen next.

Yes, he can.

Hitler is going to make a speech to the Reich at midday to-morrow. (Newspapers have already revealed this, as has also the wireless.) He will outline peace proposals—so called. These will prove to be of such a character that neither France nor England will entertain them for a moment. *Monsieur Chamberlain prendra la parole et enverra promener Monsieur Itlère, Monsieur Daladier en fera autant, et zut! la lutte s'engagera, pour de bon cette fois-ci.*

Poor de *ploo* bong? says Lady Blowfield uneasily.

Gitnik makes very rapid reply—perhaps in Hungarian, perhaps in Polish or possibly in both—which is evidently not of a reassuring character, as he ends up by stating, in English, that people in this country have not yet realised

[149]

that we are wholly vulnerable not only from the North and the East, but from the South and the West as *well*.

And what, asks Lady Blowfield faintly, about the air?

London, asserts Gitnik authoritatively, has air defences. Of that there need be no doubt at all. The provinces, on the other hand, could be attacked with the utmost ease and probably will be. It is being openly stated in Istanbul, Athens and New Mexico that a seventy-hour bombardment of Liverpool is the first item on the Nazi programme.

Lady Blowfield moans, but says nothing.

Remaining guests arrive: turn out to be Mr. and Mrs. Weatherby, whom I am not particularly pleased to meet again, but feel obliged to assume expression as of one receiving an agreeable surprise.

Gitnik immediately addresses them in Italian, to which they competently reply in French, whereupon he at once reverts to English. Weatherbys quite unperturbed, and shortly afterwards enquire whether he can tell us anything about America's attitude.

Yes, as usual, he can.

America will, for the present, keep out of the conflict. Her sympathies, however, are with the Allies. There will undoubtedly be much discussion over this business of the embargo on the sale of arms. It has been said in Rome—and Gitnik must beg of us to let this go no further—that the embargo will probably be lifted early next year.

At this Lady Blowfield looks impressed, but the Weatherbys are left cold—for which I admire them—and conviction gains strength in my own mind that Monsieur Gitnik resembles fourteenth-rate crystal-gazer, probably with business premises in mews off Tottenham Court Road.

Luncheon extremely welcome, and make determined effort to abandon the sphere of European unrest and talk about rock-gardens instead. This a dead failure.

Excellent omelette, chicken-casserole and accompaniments are silently consumed while Monsieur Gitnik, in reply to leading question from hostess—(evidently determined to Draw him Out, which is not really necessary)—tells

[151]

us that if ever he goes to Russia again, he has
been warned that he will be thrown into prison
because he Knows Too Much. Similar fate
awaits him in Germany, Esthonia and the Near
East generally, for the same reason.

Mrs. Weatherby—my opinion of her going
up every moment by leaps and bounds—declares gaily that this reminds her of a play, once
very popular, called *The Man Who Knew Too
Much*. Or does she mean *The Man Who Stayed
at Home*?

Mr. Weatherby thinks that she does. So do
I. Lady Blowfield says sadly that it matters
little now, it all seems so very far away.

Gitnik crumbles bread all over the table and
says something in unknown tongue, to which
nobody makes any immediate reply, but Lady
Blowfield's dog emits short, piercing howl.

This leads the conversation in the direction of
dogs, and I find myself giving rather maudlin
account of the charms of Robert's Benjy, wholly
adorable puppy resembling small, square wooly
bear. Mrs. Weatherby is sympathetic, Mr. W.
looks rather remote but concedes, in a detached
way, that Pekinese dogs are sometimes more

[152]

intelligent than they are given credit for being, and Lady Blowfield strokes her dog and says that he is to be evacuated to her sister's house in Hampshire next week.

Gitnik firmly recalls us to wider issues by announcing that he has received a rather curious little communication from a correspondent whose name and nationality, as we shall of course understand, he cannot disclose, and who is writing from a neutral country that must on no account be mentioned by name.

He is, however, prepared to let us see the communication if we should care to do so.

Oui, oui, replies Lady Blowfield to great agitation—evidently under the impression that this cryptic answer will wholly defeat the butler, now handing coffee and cigarettes.

(Take a good look at butler, to see what he thinks of it all, but he remains impassive.)

Coffee is finished hastily—regret this, as should much have preferred to linger—and we retreat to drawing-room and Gitnik produces from a pocket-book several newspaper cuttings —which he replaces—envelope with a foreign stamp but only looks like ordinary French one

[153]

—and postcard of which he displays one side on which is written: *"Je crois que Monsieur Hitler a les jitters."*

The rest of the card, says Gitnik, tells nothing —nothing at all. But that one phrase—coming as it does from a man who is probably better informed on the whole situation than almost anybody in Europe—that one phrase seems to him quite startlingly significant. *Non è vero?*

Everybody looks very serious, and Lady Blowfield shakes her head several times and only hopes that it's true. We all agree that we only hope it's true, and postcard is carefully replaced in pocket-book again by Monsieur Gitnik.

Shortly afterwards he evidently feels that he has shot his bolt and departs, asserting that the Ministry of Information has sent for him, but that they will not like what he feels himself obliged to say to them.

Lady Blowfield—rather wistful tone, as though not absolutely certain of her ground— enquires whether we don't think that that really is a most interesting man, and I find myself unable to emulate the Weatherbys, who main-tain a brassy silence, but make indeterminate sounds as though agreeing with her.

Take my departure at the same moment as Weatherbys, and once outside the front door Mr. W. pronounces that the wretched fellow is a complete fraud, and knows, if anything, rather less than anybody else.

Mrs. W. and I join in, and I feel more drawn towards them than I should ever have believed possible. Am sorry to note that abuse and condemnation of a common acquaintance often constitutes very strong bond of union between otherwise uncongenial spirits.

Part from them at Hyde Park Corner: Mr. W. must on no account be late—Home Office awaits him—and springs into a taxi, Mrs. W. elects to walk across the park and view dahlias, and I proceed by bus to large Oxford Street shop, where I find myself the only customer, and buy two pairs of lisle stockings to be despatched to Vicky at school.

October 6th.—Wireless reports Hitler's speech to the Reich, setting forth utterly ridiculous peace proposals. Nobody in the least interested, and wireless is switched off half-way through by Serena who says that Even the Londonderry Air, of which the B.B.C.[1] seems so fond, would be more amusing.

Agree with her in principle, and express the hope that Mr. Chamberlain will be in no hurry to reply to Adolf's nonsense. Serena thinks that he won't, and that it'll be quite fun to see what America says as their newspapers always express themselves so candidly, and asks me to serve her with a cup of coffee, a packet of cigarettes and two apples.

We then discuss at great length rumour that W.V.S.[2] is to be disbanded and started again on quite a new basis, with blue uniforms.

Mrs. Peacock asks if I would like to take over Cash Register, and I agree to do so subject to instruction, and feel important. She also suggests that I should take duty on Sunday for an hour or two as this always a difficult day on which to get help, and I light-heartedly say Yes, yes, any time she likes—I live just over the way and nothing can be easier than to step across. She can put me down for whatever

[1] British Broadcasting Corporation.
[2] Women's Voluntary Services.

hour is most difficult to fill. She immediately puts me down for 6 A.M.

October 8th.—Inclined to wish I hadn't been so obliging. Six A.M. very un-inspiring hour indeed.

Granny Bo-Peep enters Canteen at half-past seven—looks as fresh as a daisy—and tells me roguishly that my eyes are full of sleepy-dust and thinks the sand-man isn't far away, and orders breakfast—a pot of tea, buttered toast and scrambled eggs.

Colonial fellow-worker hands them to her and ejaculates—to my great annoyance—that she thinks Mrs. Winter-Gammon is just wonderful. Always cheerful, always on her feet, always thinking of others.

Granny Bo-Peep—must have preternaturally acute hearing—manages to intercept this and enquires what nonsense is that? What is there wonderful about a good-for-nothing old lady doing her bit, as the boys in brave little Belgium used to call it? Why, she's *proud* to do what she can, and if the aeroplanes do come, and a bomb drops on her—why, it just isn't going to matter. Should like, for the first time

[157]

in our association, to tell old Mrs. W.-G. that I entirely agree with her. Young Colonial—evidently nicer nature than mine—expresses suitable horror at suggested calamity, and Mrs. W.-G. is thereby encouraged to ruffle up her curls with one claw and embark on story concerning one of the stretcher-bearers who has—she alleges—attached himself to her and follows her about everywhere like a shadow. Why, she just can't imagine. (Neither can I.)

Order for Two Sausages from elderly and exhausted-looking Special Constable who has been on duty in the street all night takes me to the kitchen, where Cook expresses horror and incredulity at message and says I must have made a mistake, as nobody could order *just* sausages. He must have meant with fried bread, or mashed, or even tomatoes.

Special Constable says No, he didn't. He *said* sausages and he *meant* sausages.

Can only report this adamant spirit to Cook, who seems unable to credit it even now, and takes surreptitious look through the hatch at Special Constable, now leaning limply against the counter. He shakes his head at my suggestions of coffee, bread-and-butter or a nice cup of tea, and removes his sausages to corner of table, and Cook says it beats her how anybody can eat a sausage all on its own, let alone two of them, but she supposes it'll take all sorts to win this war.

Lull has set in and sit down on Mrs. Peacock's box and think of nineteen hundred and fourteen and myself as a V.A.D.[1] and tell myself solemnly that a quarter of a century makes a *difference* to one in many ways.

This leads on to thoughts of Robin and Vicky and I have mentally put one into khaki and the other into blue slacks, suède jacket and tin hat, when Granny Bo-Peep's voice breaks in with the assertion that she knows *just* what I'm thinking about: she can read it in my face. I'm thinking about my children.

Have scarcely ever been so near committing murder in my life.

Young Colonial—could wish she had either more discrimination or less kindliness—is encouraging old Mrs. W.-G.—who isn't in the least in need of encouraging—by respectful

[1] Voluntary Aid Detachment.

[159]

questions as to her own family circle, and Mrs.
W.-G. replies that she is alone, except for the
many, many dear friends who are good enough
to say that she means something in their lives.
She has never had children, which she implies
is an error on the part of Providence as she
knows she *ought* to have been the mother of
sons. She has a natural affinity with boys, and
they with her.

When she was living with her dear Edgar in
his East End parish, many years ago, she invariably asked him to let her teach the boys. Edgar,
she used to say, let me have the boys. Not the
girls. The boys. Just the boys. And Edgar
used to reply: These boys are the Roughest of
the Rough. They are beyond a gentlewoman's
control. But Mrs. W.-G. would simply repeat:
Give me the boys, Edgar. And Edgar—her
beloved could never hold out against her—
eventually gave her the boys. And what was the
result?

The result was that the boys—though still
the Roughest of the Rough—became tamed. A
lady's influence, was the verdict of Edgar, in
less than a month. One dear lad—a scallywag

from the dockside if ever there was one, says
Mrs. W.-G. musingly—once made use of Bad
Language in her presence. And the other poor
lads almost tore him to pieces, dear fellows.
Chivalry. Just chivalry. The Beloved always
said that she seemed to call it out.

She herself—ha-ha-ha—thinks it was because she was such A Tiny—it made them feel
protective. Little Mother Sunshine they sometimes called her—but that might have been because in those days her curlywig was gold, not
silver.

Even the young Colonial is looking rather
stunned by this time, and only ejaculates very
feebly when Mrs. W.-G. stops for breath. As
for myself, a kind of coma has overtaken me
and I find myself singing in an undertone
"South of the Border, down Mexico Way"—
to distant gramophone accompaniment.

Am relieved at Cash Register what seems like
weeks later—but is really only two hours—
and retire to Buckingham Street.

Curious sense of unreality pervades everything—cannot decide if this is due to extraordinary and unnatural way in which the war is

being conducted, without any of the developments we were all led to expect, or to lack of sleep, or merely to prolonged dose of old Mrs. Winter-Gammon's conversation.

Debate the question lying in hot bath, wake up with fearful start although am practically positive that I haven't been asleep, and think how easily I might have drowned—recollections of George Joseph Smith and Brides in the Bath follow—crawl into bed and immediately become mentally alert and completely wide awake.

This state of things endures until I get up and dress and make myself tea and hot buttered toast.

Timid tap at flat door interrupts me, and, to my great surprise, find Muriel—curls and all—outside. She explains that Serena has said that I have a bathroom and that I am very kind and that there is no doubt whatever of my allowing her to have a bath. Is this all right?

Am touched and flattered by this trusting spirit, and assure her that it is.

(*Query:* Are my services to the Empire in the present world-war to take the form of

[162]

supplying hot baths to those engaged in more responsible activities? *Answer:* At present, apparently, yes.)

Muriel comes out from bathroom more decorative than ever—curls evidently natural ones —and we have agreeable chat concerning all our fellow workers, about whom our opinions tally. She then drifts quietly out again, saying that she is going to have a really *marvellous* time this afternoon, because she and a friend of hers have been saving up all their petrol and they are actually going to drive out to Richmond Park. Remembrance assails me, after she has gone, that Serena has said that Muriel's parents own a Rolls-Royce and are fabulously wealthy. Have dim idea of writing short, yet brilliant, article, on New Values in Wartime —but nothing comes of it.

Instead, write a letter to Robert—not short, but not brilliant either. Also instructions to Aunt Blanche about letting Cook have the Sweep, if that's what she wants, and suggesting blackberry jelly if sugar will run to it, and not allowing her, on any account, to make pounds and pounds of marrow jam which she

[163]

is certain to suggest and which everybody hates
and refuses to touch.

P.S.: I have seen Mrs. Winter-Gammon
quite a lot, and she seems very energetic indeed
and has sent Aunt Blanche her love. Can quite
understand why Aunt Blanche has said that she
will not agree to share a flat with her again
when the war is over. Mrs. W.-G. has dynamic
personality and is inclined to have a devitalising
effect on her surroundings.

Re-read postscript and am not at all sure that
it wouldn't have been better to say in plain English that old Mrs. W.-G. is more aggravating
than ever, and Aunt Blanche is well out of shar-
ing a flat with her.

Ring up Rose later on and enquire whether
she has yet got a job.

No, nothing like that. Rose has sent in her
name and qualifications to the British Medical
Association, and has twice been round to see
them, and she has received and filled in several
forms, and has also had a letter asking if she is
prepared to serve with His Majesty's Forces
abroad with the rank of Major, and has humorously replied Yes certainly, if H. M. Forces

don't mind about her being a woman, and there the question, at present, remains.

All Rose's medical colleagues are equally unoccupied and she adds that the position of the Harley Street obstetricians is particularly painful, as all their prospective patients have evacuated themselves from London and the prospect of their talents being utilised by the Services is naturally non-existent.

What, asks Rose, about myself?

Make the best show I can with the Canteen —position on Cash Register obviously quite a responsible one in its way—but Rose simply replies that it's too frightful the way we're all hanging about wasting our time and doing nothing whatever.

Retire from this conversation deeply depressed.

October 9th.—Mrs. Peacock electrifies entire Canteen by saying that she has met a man who says that the British Government is going to accept Hitler's peace terms.

Can only reply that he must be the only man in England to have adopted this view—and this is supported by everyone within hearing, Serena going so far as to assert that man must be a Nazi propaganda-agent as nobody else could have thought of anything so absurd.

Mrs. P. looks rather crushed, but is not at all resentful, only declaring that man is *not* a Nazi propaganda-agent, but she thinks perhaps he just said it so as to be unlike anybody else— in which he has succeeded.

Man forthwith dismissed from the conversation by everybody.

No further incident marks the day until supper-time, when customary uproar of radio, gramophone, darts contest and newly imported piano (situated just outside Women's Restroom) has reached its climax.

Ginger-headed stretcher-bearer then comes up to order two fried eggs, two rashers, one sausage-roll and a suet dumpling, and asks me if I've heard the latest.

Prepare to be told that Dr. Goebbels has been executed at the behest of his Führer at the very least, but news turns out to be less sensational. It is to the effect that the underworld has now been issued with shrouds, to be kept in the back of each car. Am dreadfully inclined to laugh at

Has now been issued with shrouds.

this, but stretcher-bearer is gloom personified, and I feel that my reaction is most unsuitable and immediately stifle it.

Stretcher-bearer then reveals that his chief feeling at this innovation is one of resentment. He was, he declares, in the last war, and nobody had shrouds *then*, but he supposes that this is to be a regular Gentleman's Business.

Condole with him as best I can, and he takes his supper and walks away with it, still muttering very angrily about shrouds.

October 10th.—Letter received from extremely distinguished woman, retired from important Civil Service post less than a year ago, and with whom I am only in a position to claim acquaintance at all because she is friend of Rose's. She enquires—very dignified phraseology—if I can by any chance tell her of suitable war work.

Can understand use of the word suitable when she adds, though without apparent rancour, entire story of recent attempts to serve her country through the medium of local A.R.P.[1] where she lives. She has filled up num-

[1] Air Raid Precautions.

bers of forms, and been twice interviewed by very refined young person of about nineteen, and finally summoned to nearest Council Offices for work alleged to be in need of experienced assistance.

Work takes the form of sitting in very chilly entrance-hall of Council Offices directing enquirers to go Upstairs and To the Right for information about Fuel Control, and Downstairs and Straight Through for Food Regulations.

Adds—language still entirely moderate—that she can only suppose the hall porter employed by Council Offices has just been called up.

Am shocked and regretful, but in no position to offer any constructive suggestion.

Letter also reaches me from Cook—first time we have ever corresponded—saying that Winnie's mother has sent a message that Winnie's young sister came back from school with earache which has now gone to her foot and they think it may be rheumatic fever and can Winnie be spared for a bit to help. Cook adds that she supposes the girl had better go, and adds *P.S.*:

The Butcher has took Winnie and dropped her the best part of the way. *P.P.S.:* Madam, what about the Sweep?

Am incredibly disturbed by this communication on several counts. Winnie's absence more than inconvenient, and Cook herself will be the first person to complain of it bitterly. Have no security that Winnie's mother's idea of "a bit" will correspond with mine.

Cannot understand why no letter from Aunt Blanche. Can Cook have made entire arrangement without reference to her? Allusion to Sweep also utterly distracting. Why so soon again? Or, alternatively, did Aunt Blanche omit to summon him at Cook's original request, made almost immediately after my departure? If so, for what reason, and why have I been told nothing?

Can think of nothing else throughout very unsatisfactory breakfast, prepared by myself, in which electric toaster alternately burns the bread or produces no impression on it whatever except for three pitch-black perpendicular lines.

Tell myself that I am being foolish, and that all will be cleared up in the course of a post or

[169]

two, and settle down resolutely to Inside Information column of favourite daily paper, which I read through five times only to find myself pursuing long, imaginary conversation with Cook at the end of it all.

Decide that the only thing to do is to telephone to Aunt Blanche this morning and clear up entire situation.

Resume Inside Information.

Decide that telephoning is not only expensive, but often unsatisfactory as well, and letter will serve the purpose better.

Begin Inside Information all over again.

Imaginary conversation resumed, this time with Aunt Blanche.

Decide to telephone, and immediately afterwards decide not to telephone.

Telephone bell rings and strong intuitional flash comes over me that decision has been taken out of my hands. (Just as well.)

Yes?

Am I Covent Garden? says masculine voice.

No, I am not.

Masculine voice ejaculates—tone expressive of annoyance, rather than regret for having disturbed me—and conversation closes.

Mysterious unseen compulsion causes me to dial TRU and ask for home number.

Die now cast.

After customary buzzing and clicking, Robert's voice says Yes? and is told by Exchange to go ahead.

We do go ahead and I say Is he all right? to which he replies, sounding rather surprised, that he's quite all right. Are the children, Aunt Blanche and the maids all right? What about Winnie?

Robert says, rather vaguely, that he believes Winnie has gone home for a day or two, but they seem to be Managing, and do I want anything special?

Answer in the weakest possible way that I only wanted to know if they were All Right, and Robert again reiterates that they are and that he will be writing to-night, but this A.R.P.[1] business takes up a lot of time. He hopes the Canteen work is proving interesting and not too tiring, and he thinks that Hitler is beginning to find out that he's been playing a mug's game.

So do I, and am just about to elaborate this

[1] Air Raid Precautions.

theme when I remember the Sweep and enquire if I can speak to Aunt Blanche.

Robert replies that he thinks she's in the bath.

Telephone pips three times, and he adds that, if that's all, perhaps we'd better ring off.

Entire transaction strikes me as having been unsatisfactory in the extreme.

October 11th.—Nothing from Aunt Blanche except uninformative picture postcard of Loch in Scotland—in which I take no interest whatever—with communication to the effect that the trees are turning colour and looking lovely and she has scarcely ever before seen so *many* hollyberries out *so early*. The children brought in some beautiful branches of beech-leaves on Sunday and Aunt Blanche hopes to put them in glycerine so that they will last in the house for *months*. The news seems to her good *on the whole*. The Russians evidently *not* anxious for war, and Hitler, did he but know it, *up a gumtree*. Much love.

Spend much time debating question as to whether I had not better go home for the weekend.

October 12th.—Decide finally to ask Mrs. Peacock whether I can be spared for ten days in order to go home on urgent private affairs. Am unreasonably reluctant to make this suggestion in spite of telling myself what is undoubtedly the fact: that Canteen will easily survive my absence without disaster.

Mrs. Peacock proves sympathetic but tells me that application for leave will have to be made direct to Commandant. Can see she expects me to receive this announcement with dismay, so compel myself to reply Certainly, with absolute composure.

(Do not believe that she is taken in for one second.)

Debate inwardly whether better to tackle Commandant instantly, before having time to dwell on it, or wait a little and get up more spirit. Can see, however, that latter idea is simply craven desire to postpone the interview and must not on any account be entertained seriously.

Serena enters Canteen just as I am preparing to brace myself and exclaims that I look very green in the face, do I feel ill?

Certainly not. I am perfectly well. Does

Serena know if Commandant is in her office, as I wish to speak to her.

Oh, says Serena, that accounts for my looks. Yes, she is.

I say Good, in very resolute tone, and go off. Fragmentary quotations from Charge of the Light Brigade come into my mind, entirely of their own accord.

Serena runs after me and says she'll come too, and is it anything very awful?

Not at all. It is simply that I feel my presence to be temporarily required at home, and am proposing to go down there for ten days. This scheme to be subjected to Commandant's approval as a mere matter of courtesy.

At this Serena laughs so much that I find myself laughing also, though perhaps less wholeheartedly, and I enquire whether Serena supposes Commandant will make a fuss? Serena replies, cryptically, that it won't exactly be a fuss, but she's sure to be utterly odious—which is precisely what I anticipate myself.

Temporary respite follows, as Serena, after pressing her nose against glass panel of office window, reports Commandant to be engaged in tearing two little Red Cross nurses limb from limb.

Cannot feel that this bodes well for me, but remind myself vigorously that I am old enough to be Commandant's mother and that, if necessary, shall have no hesitation in telling her so.

(*Query:* Would it impress her if I did? *Answer:* No.)

Office door flies open and Red Cross nurse comes out, but leaves fellow victim within.

Serena and I, with one voice, enquire what is happening, and are told in reply that Her Highness is gone off of the deep end, that's what. Long and very involved story follows of which nothing is clear to me except that Red Cross nurse declares that she isn't going to be told by anyone that she doesn't know her job, and have we any of us ever heard of Lord Horder?

Yes, we not unnaturally have.

Then who was it, do we suppose, who told her himself that he never wished to see better work in the ward than what hers was?

Office door, just as she is about to reply to this rhetorical question, flies open once more and second white veil emerges, which throws first one into still more agitation and they walk away arm-in-arm, but original informant suddenly turns her head over her shoulder and finishes up reference to Lord Horder with very distinctly-enunciated monosyllable: E.

Serena and I giggle and Commandant, from within the office, calls out to someone unseen to shut that door *at once*, there's far too much noise going on and is this a girls' school, or an Organisation of national importance?

Should like to reply that it's neither.

Rather draughty pause ensues, and I ask Serena if she knows how the underworld manages to be chilly and stuffy at one and the same time—but she doesn't.

Suggests that I had better knock at the door, which I do, and get no reply.

Harder, says Serena.

I make fresh attempt, again unsuccessful, and am again urged to violence by Serena. Third effort is much harder than I meant it to be and sounds like onslaught from a battering-ram. It produces a very angry command to Come In! and I do so.

Commandant is, as usual, smoking and writing her head off at one and the same time, and continues her activities without so much as a glance in my direction.

I contemplate the back of her head—coat collar wants brushing—and reflect that I could (*a*) throw something at her—nearest available missile is cardboard gas-mask container, which I don't think heavy enough; (*b*) walk out again; (*c*) tell her clearly and coldly that I have No Time to Waste.

Am bracing myself for rather modified form of (*c*) when she snaps out enquiry as to what I want.

I want to leave London for a week or ten days.

Commandant snaps again. This time it is Why.

Because my presence is required in my own house in Devonshire.

Devonshire? replies Commandant in offensively incredulous manner. What do I mean by Devonshire?

Cannot exactly explain why, but at this precise moment am suddenly possessed by spirit of defiance and hear myself replying in superbly

detached tones that I am not here to waste
either her time or my own and should be much
obliged if she would merely note that I shall
not be giving my services at Canteen for the
next ten days.

Am by no means certain that thunderbolt
from Heaven will not strike me where I stand
but it is withheld, and sensation of great ex-
hilaration descends upon me instead.

Commandant looks at me—first time she has
ever done so in the whole of our association—
and says in tones of ice that I *am* wasting her
time, as the Canteen Time-Sheet is entirely in
the hands of Mrs. Peacock and I ought to have
made my application for leave through her.

She then slams rubber stamp violently onto
inoffensive piece of paper and turns her back
again.

I rejoin Serena, to whom I give full account
of entire episode—probably too full, as Serena
—after highly commending me—says that I
couldn't have made half such a long speech in
the time. Realise that I couldn't, and that
imagination has led me astray, and withdraw
about half of what I have told her, but the other

half accurate and much applauded by Serena and subsequently by Mrs. Peacock.

Mrs. P. also says that Of course I must go home, and Devonshire sounds lovely, and she wishes she lived there herself. Do I know Ilfracombe? Yes, quite well. Does Mrs. Peacock? No, but she's always heard that it's lovely. I agree that it is, and conversation turns to macaroni-and-tomato, again on the menu to-night, bacon now off, and necessity of holding back the brown bread as it will be wanted for to-morrow's breakfast.

Serena orders coffee and stands drinking it, and says that there is to be a lecture on Fractures at midnight. I ask why midnight, and she replies vaguely, Oh, because they think it'll be dark then.

Am unable to follow this, and do not attempt to do so.

News percolates through Canteen—cannot at all say how—that I am going to Devonshire for ten days and fellow workers tell me how fortunate I am, and enquire whether I know Moretonhampstead, Plymouth Hoe, and the road between Axminster and Charmouth.

[179]

Old Granny Bo-Peep appears as usual—have strong suspicion that she never leaves the underworld at all, but stays there all day and all night—and romps up to me with customary air of roguish enjoyment.

What is this, she asks, that a little bird has just told her? That one of our very latest recruits is looking back from the plough already? But that's only her fun—she's delighted, really, to hear that I'm to have a nice holiday in the country. All the way down to Devon, too! Right away from the war, and hard work, and a lovely rest amongst the birds and the flowers.

Explain without any enthusiasm that my presence is required at home and that I am obliged to take long and probably crowded journey in order to look into various domestic problems, put them in order, and then return to London as soon as I possibly can.

Old Mrs. W.-G. says she quite understands, in highly incredulous tones, and proceeds to a long speech concerning her own ability to work for days and nights at a stretch without ever requiring any rest at all. As for taking a holiday—well, such a thing never occurs to her.

[180]

It just simply doesn't ever cross her mind. It isn't that she's exactly stronger than anybody else—on the contrary, she's always been supposed to be rather fragile—but while there's work to be done, she just has to do it, and the thought of rest never occurs to her.

Beloved Edgar used to say to her: One day you'll break down. You *must* break down. You cannot possibly go on like this and *not* break down. But she only laughed and went on just the same. She's always been like that, and she hopes she always will be.

Feel sure that hope will probably be realised.

Evening proceeds as usual. Mock air-raid alarm is given at ten o'clock, and have the gratification of seeing Serena race for her tin hat and fly back with it on her head, looking very *affairée* indeed.

Canteen workers, who are not expected to take any part in manœuvres, remain at their posts and seize opportunity to drink coffee, clear the table, and tell one another that we are all to be disbanded quite soon and placed under the Home Office—that we are all to be given the sack—that we are all to be put into blue dun-

garees at a cost of eleven shillings per head—
and similar pieces of intelligence.

Stretcher-bearers presently reappear and story
goes round that imaginary casualty having been
placed on stretcher and left there with feet
higher than his head, has been taken off to First
Aid Post in a dead faint and hasn't come round
yet.

Rather sharp words pass between one of the
cooks and young Canteen voluntary helper in
flowered cretonne overall, who declares that her
orders are not receiving proper attention. Cook
asserts that *all* orders are taken in rotation and
Flowered Cretonne replies No, hers aren't.
Deadlock appears to have been reached and
they glare at one another through the hatch.

Two more cooks in background of kitchen
come nearer in support of colleague, or else in
hopes of excitement, but Cretonne Overall contents herself with repeating that she must say
it seems rather extraordinary, and then retiring
to tea-urn, which I think feeble.

She asks for a cup of tea—very strong and
plenty of sugar—which I give her and tells
me that she doesn't think this place is properly

run, just look how the floor wants sweeping, and I am impelled to point out that there is nothing to prevent her from taking a broom and putting this right at once.

Cretonne Overall gives me a look of concentrated hatred, snatches up her cup of tea and walks away with it to furthest table in the room. Can see her throwing occasional glances of acute dislike in my direction throughout remainder of the night.

Serena returns—tells me that the feature of the practice has been piled-up bodies and that these have amused themselves by hooking their legs and arms together quite inextricably and giving the first-aid men a good deal of trouble, but everyone has seen the funny side of it and it's been a very merry evening altogether.

Better, she adds gloomily, than the concert which we are promised for next week is likely to be.

She then drinks two cups of coffee, eats half a bar of chocolate and a banana, and announces that she is going to bed.

Presently my relief arrives: tiny little creature with bobbed brown hair, who has taken duty from 10 P.M. to 10 A.M. every night since war started. I express admiration at her self-sacrifice, and she says No, it's nothing, because she isn't a voluntary worker at all—she gets paid.

As this no doubt means that she is working part of the day as well, can only feel that grounds for admiration are, if anything, re-doubled and tell her so, but produce no effect whatever, as she merely replies that there's nothing to praise her for, she gets paid.

She adds, however, that it is a satisfaction to her to be doing something Against that Man. She said to Dad at the very beginning: Dad, I want to do something *against* him. So she took this job, and she put herself down at the Hospital for blood-transfusion, and they've took some from her already and will be wanting more later. In this way, she repeats, she can feel she's doing something *Against Him*—which is what she wants.

As much struck by contrast between her appearance—tiny little thing, with very pretty smile—and extreme ferocity of her sentiments.

We exchange Good-nights and I collect my

[184]

coat from Women's Rest-room where it hangs
on a peg, in the midst of camp-beds.

On one of them, under mountain of coverings,
huge mop of curls is just visible—no doubt
belonging to Muriel.

Serena is sitting bolt upright on adjacent
bed, legs straight out in front of her in surely
very uncomfortable position, writing letters.
This seems to me most unnatural hour at which
to conduct her correspondence, which apparently consists largely of picture postcards.

Wireless outside is emitting jazz with tre-
mendous violence, engines are running, and a
group of persons with surely very loud voices
are exchanging views about the Archbishop of
York. They are of opinion, after listening to
His Grace's broadcast the other night, that
Where a Man like that is wanted is In the
Cabinet.

Agree with them, and should like to go out
and say so, adding suggestion that he would
make first-class Prime Minister—but Serena intervenes with plaintive observation that, as they
all agree with one another and keep on saying
That's Right, she can't imagine why they *must*

go on discussing it instead of letting her get
a little sleep.

At this I feel the moment has come for speech
which I have long wished to deliver, and I
suggest to Serena that she has undertaken a
form of war service which is undoubtedly going
to result in her speedy collapse from want of
sleep, fresh air, and properly-regulated existence
generally. Wouldn't it be advisable to do something more rational?

There *isn't* anything, says Serena positively.
Nobody wants anybody to do anything, and
yet if they do nothing they go mad.

Can see that it will take very little to send
Serena into floods of tears, and have no wish
to achieve this result, or to emulate Darling's
methods with Commandant, so simply tell her
that I suppose she knows her own business best
—(not that I do, for one minute)—and depart from the underworld.

October 13th.—Countryside bears out all that
Aunt Blanche has written of its peaceful appearance, autumn colouring, and profusion of
scarlet berries prematurely decorating the holly-
trees.

[186]

Train very crowded and arrives thirty-five minutes late, and I note that my feelings entirely resemble those of excited small child returning home for the holidays. Robert has said that he cannot meet me owing to A.R.P.[1] duties but is there at the station, and seems pleased by my return, though saying nothing openly to that effect.

We drive home—everything looks lovely and young colt in Home Farm field has miraculously turned into quite tall black horse. Tell Robert that I feel as if I had been away for years, and he replies that it is two and a half weeks since I left.

I ask after the evacuees, the puppy, Aunt Blanche, Cook and the garden and tell Robert about Serena, the Canteen, the Blowfields and their cosmopolitan friend—Robert of opinion that he ought to be interned at once—and unresponsive attitude of the Ministry of Information.

What does Robert think about Finland? Envoy now in Moscow. Robert, in reply, tells me what he thinks, not about Finland, but

[1] Air Raid Precautions.

about Stalin. Am interested, but not in any way surprised, having heard it all before a great many times.

As we drive in at the gate Marigold and Margery dart round the house—and I have brief, extraordinary hallucination of having returned to childish days of Robin and Vicky. Cannot possibly afford to dwell on this illusion for even one second, and get out of the car with such haste that suitcase falls with me and most of its contents are scattered on the gravel, owing to defective lock.

Robert not very pleased.

Marigold and Margery look pink and cheerful, Miss Doreen Fitzgerald comes up from garden, knitting, and says I'm Very Welcome, certainly I am. (Should never be surprised if she offered to show me my room.)

Winnie appears at hall door, at which I exclaim, Oh, are you back, Winnie? and then feel it would be no more than I deserve if she answered No, she's in Moscow with the Finnish Envoy at the Kremlin—but this flight of satire fortunately does not occur to her, and she smiles very cheerfully and says, Yes, Mum thought it might be a long job with Bessie, and if she found she couldn't manage, she'd send for Winnie again later on.

Can think of no more unsatisfactory arrangement, from domestic point of view, but hear myself assuring Winnie cordially that that'll be quite all right.

We all collect various properties from the gravel, and Benjy achieves *succés fou* with evacuees and myself by snatching up bedroom slipper and prancing away with it under remotest of the lilac bushes, from whence he looks out at us with small growls, whilst shaking slipper between his teeth.

Marigold and Margery scream with laughter and applaud him heartily under pretence of rescuing slipper, and Aunt Blanche comes downstairs and picks up my sponge and then greets me most affectionately.

Am still pursuing scattered belongings, rolled to distant points of the compass, when small car dashes in at the gate and I have only time to tell Aunt Blanche to get rid of them *whoever* it is, and hasten into the house.

(They cannot possibly have failed to see me,

but could they perhaps think, owing to unfamiliar London clothes, that I am newly arrived visitor with eccentric preference for
unpacking just outside the hall door? Can
only hope so, without very much confidence.)

Hasten upstairs—rapturously delighted at
familiar bedroom once more—and am moved
at finding particularly undesirable green glass
vase with knobs, that I have never liked, placed
on dressing-table and containing two yellow
dahlias, one branch of pallid Michaelmas
daisies, and some belated sprigs of catmint—
undoubted effort of Marigold and Margery.

Snatch off hat and coat—can hear Aunt
Blanche under the window haranguing unknown
arrivals—and resort to looking-glass, brush and
comb, lipstick and powder-puff, but find myself
breaking off all operations to straighten favourite Cézanne reproduction hanging on the walls,
and also restoring small clock to *left*-hand corner of table where I left it, and from which it
has been moved to the right.

(*Query:* Does this denote unusually orderly
mind and therefore rank as an asset, or is it
merely quality vulgarly—and often inaccu-

rately—known to my youth as old-maidish-ness?)

Sounds of car driving away again—look out of the window, but am none the wiser except for seeing number on the rear-plate, which conveys nothing, and Benjy now openly chewing up slipper-remains.

Ejaculate infatuatedly that he is a little lamb, and go downstairs to tea.

This laid in dining-room and strikes me as being astonishingly profuse, and am rendered speechless when Aunt Blanche says Dear, dear, they've forgotten the honey, and despatches Marigold to fetch it. She also apologises for scarcity of butter—can only say that it hadn't struck me, as there must be about a quarter of a pound per head in the dish—but adds that at least we can have as much clotted cream as we like, and we shall have to make the best of that.

We do.

She asks after Serena Fiddlededee—am able to respond enthusiastically and say we've made great friends and that Serena is so amusing—and then mentions Pussy Winter-Gammon. Totally different atmosphere at once becomes noticeable, and although I only reply that she seems to be very well indeed and full of energy, Aunt Blanche makes deprecatory sort of sound with her tongue, frowns heavily and exclaims that Pussy—not that she wants to say anything against her—really is a perfect fool, and enough to try the patience of a saint. What on earth she wants to behave in that senseless way for, at her time of life, Aunt Blanche doesn't pretend to understand, but there it is—Pussy Winter-Gammon always has been inclined to be thoroughly tiresome. Aunt Blanche is, if I know what she means, devoted to Pussy but, at the same time, able to recognise her faults.

Can foresee that Aunt Blanche and I are going to spend hours discussing old Mrs. W.-G. and her faults.

I enquire what the car was, and am told it was Nothing Whatever, only a man and his wife who suggested that we should like to give them photographs from which they propose to evolve exquisitely-finished miniatures, painted on ivorine, suitably framed, to be purchased by us for the sum of five guineas each.

Ask how Aunt Blanche got rid of them and

[192]

she seems reluctant to reply, but at last admits that she told them that we ourselves didn't want any miniatures at the moment but that they might go on down the road, turn to the left, and call on Lady Boxe.

The butler, adds Aunt Blanche hurriedly, will certainly know how to get rid of them.

Cannot pretend to receive the announcement of this unscrupulous proceeding with anything but delighted amusement.

It also leads to my asking for news of Lady B.'s present activities and hearing that she still talks of a Red Cross Hospital—officers only—but that it has not so far materialised. Lady B.'s Bentley, however, displays a Priority label on wind-screen, and she has organized First Aid classes for the village.

At this I exclaim indignantly that we all attended First Aid classes all last winter, under conditions of the utmost discomfort, sitting on tiny chairs in front of minute desks in the Infant School, as being only available premises. What in the name of common sense do we want *more* First Aid for?

Aunt Blanche shakes her head and says Yes,

she knows all that, but there it is. People are interested in seeing the inside of a large house, and they get coffee and biscuits, and there you are.

I tell Aunt Blanche that, if it wasn't for Stalin and his general behaviour, I should almost certainly become a Communist to-morrow. Not a Bolshevik, surely? says Aunt Blanche. Yes, a Bolshevik—at least to the extent of beheading quite a number of the idle rich.

On thinking this over, perceive that the number really boils down to one—and realise that my political proclivities are of a biassed and personal character, and not worth a moment's consideration. (*Note:* Say no more about them.)

Tea is succeeded by Happy Families with infant evacuees Marigold and Margery, again recalling nursery days now long past of Robin and Vicky.

Both are eventually despatched to bed, and I see that the moment has come for visiting Cook in the kitchen. Remind myself how splendidly she behaved at outbreak of war, and that Aunt Blanche has said she thinks things *are* all right, but am nevertheless apprehensive.

Have hardly set foot in the kitchen before realising—do not know how or why—that apprehensions are about to be justified. Start off nevertheless with *faux air* of confident cheerfulness, and tell Cook that I'm glad to be home again, glad to see that Winnie's back at work, glad to see how well the children look, very glad indeed to see that she herself doesn't look too tired. Cannot think of anything else to be glad about, and come to a stop.

Cook, in very sinister tones, hopes that I've enjoyed my holiday.

Well, it hasn't been exactly a *holiday*.

(Should like to tell her that I have been engaged, day and night, on activities of national importance but this totally unsupported by fact, and do not care to mention Canteen which would not impress Cook, who knows the extent of my domestic capabilities, in the very least.)

Instead, ask weakly if everything has been All Right?

Cook says Yes'm, in tones which mean No'm, and at once adds that she's been on the go from morning till night, and of course the nursery makes a great deal of extra work and that girl Winnie has no head at all. She's not a *bad* girl, in her way, but she hasn't a head. She never will have, in Cook's opinion.

I express concern at this deficiency, and also regret that Winnie, with or without head, should have had to be away.

As to that, replies Cook austerely, it may or may not have been necessary. All *she* knows is that she had to be up and on her hands and knees at half-past five every morning, to see to that there blessed kitchen range.

(If this was really so, can only say that Cook has created a precedent, as no servant in this house has ever, in any circumstances, dreamed of coming downstairs before a quarter to seven at the very earliest—Cook herself included.)

The range, continues Cook, has been more trying than she cares to say. She does, however, say—and again describes herself at half-past five every morning, on her hands and knees. (Cannot see that this extraordinary position could have been in any way necessary, or even desirable.)

There is, in Cook's opinion, Something Wrong with the Range. Make almost automatic reply

She had to be up and on her hands and knees at half-past five every morning to see to that there range.

to this well-worn domestic plaint, to the effect that it must be the flues, but Cook repudiates the flues altogether and thinks it's something more like the whole range *gone*, if I know what she means.

I do know what she means, only too well, and assure her that a new cooking-stove is quite out of the question at present and that I regret it as much as she does. Cook obviously doesn't believe me and we part in gloom and constraint.

Am once again overcome by the wide divergence between fiction and fact, and think of faithful servant Hannah in the March family and how definite resemblance between her behaviour and Cook's was quite discernible at outbreak of war, but is now no longer noticeable in any way. All would be much easier if Cook's conduct rather more consistent, and would remain preferably on Hannah-level, or else definitely below it—but *not* veering from one to the other.

Make these observations in condensed form to Robert and he asks Who is Hannah? and looks appalled when I say that Hannah is character from the classics. Very shortly afterwards he goes into the study and I have recourse to Aunt Blanche.

She is equally unresponsive about Hannah, but says Oh yes, she knows *Little Women* well, only she can't remember anybody called Hannah, and am I sure I don't mean Aunt March? And anyway, books are no guide to real life.

Abandon all literary by-paths and come into the open with straightforward enquiry as to the best way of dealing with Cook.

Give her a week's holiday, advises Aunt Blanche instantly. A week will make all the difference. She and I and Winnie can manage the cooking between us, and perhaps Doreen Fitzgerald would lend a hand.

Later on I decide to adopt this scheme, with modifications—eliminating all assistance from Aunt Blanche, Winnie and Doreen Fitzgerald and sending for Mrs. Vallence—once kitchen-maid to Lady Frobisher—from the village.

October 15th.—We plough the fields and scatter, at Harvest Home service, and church is smothered in flowers, pumpkins, potatoes, apples and marrows. The infant Margery pulls my skirt—which is all she can reach—and mut-

ters long, hissing communication of which I
hear not one word and whisper back in dismay:
Does she want to be taken out?

She shakes her head.

I nod mine in return, to imply that I quite
understand whatever it was she meant to convey, and hope she will be satisfied—but she
isn't, and hisses again.

This time it is borne in on me that she is
saying it was she who placed the largest marrow—which is much bigger than she is herself
—in position near the organ-pipes, and I nod
very vigorously indeed, and gaze admiringly at
the marrow.

Margery remains with her eyes glued to it
throughout the service.

Note that no single member of the congre-
gation is carrying gas-mask, and ask Robert
afterwards if he thinks the omission matters,
and he says No.

Our Vicar is encouraging from the pulpit—
sensation pervades entire church when one
R.A.F.[1] uniform and one military one walk
in and we recognise, respectively, eldest son

[1] Royal Air Force.

of the butcher and favourite nephew of Mrs. Vallence—and strange couple in hiker's attire appear in pew belonging to aged Farmer (who has been bed-ridden for years and never comes to church) and are viewed with most un-Christian disfavour by everybody. (Presumable exception must here be made, however, in favour of Our Vicar.)

Exchange customary greetings outside with neighbours, take automatic glance—as usual—at corner beneath yew-tree where I wish to be deposited in due course and register hope that Nazi bombs may not render this impracticable—and glean the following items of information:

Johnnie Lamb from Water Lane Cottages, has *gone*.

(Sounds very final indeed, but really means training-camp near Salisbury.)

Most of the other boys haven't yet Gone, but are anxious to Go, and expect to do so at any minute.

Bill Chuff, who was in the last war, got hisself taken at once and is said by his wife to be guarding the Power Station at Devonport. (Can only say, but do not of course do so, that Bill

Chuff will have to alter his ways quite a lot if he is to be a success at the Power Station at Devonport. Should be interested to hear what Our Vicar, who has spent hours in spiritual wrestling with Bill Chuff in the past fifteen years, thinks of this appointment.)

An aeroplane was seen over the mill, flying very low, three days ago, and had a foreign look about it—but it didn't *do* anything, so may have been Belgian. Cannot attempt to analyse the component parts of this statement and simply reply, Very Likely.

Lady B. has sent up to say that she will employ any girl who has passed her First Aid Examination, in future Red Cross Hospital, and has met with hardly any response as a rumour has gone round that she intends to make everybody else scrub the floors and do the cooking while she manages all the nursing.

Am quite prepared to believe this, and manage to convey as much without saying it in so many words.

Gratified at finding myself viewed as a great authority on war situation, and having many enquiries addressed to me.

What is going to happen about Finland, and

do I think that Russia is playing a Double Game? (To this I reply, Triple, at the very least.)

Can I perhaps say where the British Army is, exactly?

If I can't, it doesn't matter, but it would be a Comfort to know whether it has really moved up to the Front yet, or not. The Ministry of Information doesn't *tell* one much, does it?

No, it doesn't.

Then what, in my opinion, is it *for*?

To this, can only return an evasive reply.

The village of Mandeville Fitzwarren, into which Mrs. Greenslade's Ivy married last year, hasn't had a single gas-mask issued to it yet, and is much disturbed, because this looks as though it was quite Out of the World, which isn't the case at all.

Promise to lay the case of Mandeville Fitzwarren before Robert in his official A.R.P.[1] capacity without delay.

(M. F. is minute cluster of six cottages, a farm, inn and post-office, in very remote valley concealed in a labyrinth of tiny lanes and ut-

[1] Air Raid Precautions.

terly invisible from anywhere at all, including the sky.)

Final enquiry is whether Master Robin is nineteen yet, and when I reply that he isn't, everybody expresses satisfaction and hopes It'll be Over before he's finished his schooling.

Am rather overcome and walk to the car, where all emotion is abruptly dispersed by astonishing sight of cat Thompson sitting inside it, looking out of the window.

Evacuees Marigold and Margery, who are gazing at him with admiration, explain that he followed them all the way from home and they didn't know what else to do with him, so shut him into the car. Accordingly drive back with Thompson sitting on my knee and giving me sharp, severe scratch when Robert sounds horn at the corner.

Peaceful afternoon ensues, write quantity of letters, and Aunt Blanche says it is a great relief not to have to read the newspapers, and immerses herself in *Letters of Miss Weeton* instead and says they are so restful.

Tell her that I have read them all through three times already and find them entrancing, but not a bit restful. Doesn't Aunt Barton's behaviour drive her to a frenzy, and what about Brother Tom's?

Aunt Blanche only replies, in thoroughly abstracted tones, that poor little Miss Pedder has just caught fire and is in a fearful blaze, and will I please not interrupt her till she sees what happens next.

Can only leave Aunt Blanches to enjoy her own idea of restful literature.

Finish letters—can do nothing about Cook owing to nation-wide convention that employers do not Speak on a Sunday in any circumstance whatever—decide that this will be a good moment to examine my wardrobe—am much discouraged by the result—ask Robert if he would like a walk and he says No, not now, this is his one opportunity of going through his accounts.

As Robert is leaning back in study armchair in front of the fire, with *Blackwood's Magazine* on his knees, I think it tactful to withdraw.

Reflect on the number of times I have told myself that even *one* hour of leisure would enable me to mend arrears of shoulder-straps and stockings, wash gloves, and write long letter to

Robert's mother in South of France, and then instantly retire to drawing-room fire and arm-chair opposite to Aunt Blanche's, and am only roused by ringing of gong for tea.

Evening is spent in playing Spillikins with evacuees, both of whom are highly skilled performers, and leave Aunt Blanche and myself standing at the post.

Eleven o'clock has struck and I am half-way to bed before I remember Mandeville Fitzwarren and go down again and lay before Robert eloquent exposition of the plight of its inhabitants.

Robert not at all sympathetic—he has had several letters from Mandeville Fitzwarren, and has personally addressed a Meeting of its fourteen parishioners, and assured them that they have not been forgotten. In the meantime, he declares, nobody is in the least likely to come and bomb them from the air, and they need not think it. It's all conceit.

This closes the discussion.

October 16th.—Very exhausting debate between myself and Cook.

I tell her—pleasant tone, bright expression,

firmness mingled with benevolence—that she has thoroughly earned a rest and that I should like her to take at least a week's holiday whilst I am at home. Wednesday, I should suggest, would be a good day for her to go.

Cook immediately assumes an air of profound offence and says Oh no'm, that isn't at all necessary. *She* doesn't want any holiday.

Yes, I say, she does. It will do her good.

Cook shakes her head and gives superior smile, quite devoid of mirth.

Yes, Cook, really.

No'm. It's very kind of me, but she couldn't think of such a thing.

But we could manage, I urge—at which Cook looks highly incredulous and rather resentful—and I should *like* her to have a holiday, and I feel sure she *needs* a holiday.

Cook returns, unreasonably, that she is too tired for a holiday to do her any good. She wouldn't enjoy it.

In another moment we are back at the stove *motif* again, and I am once more forced to hear of Cook's suspicion that something is wrong with it, that she thinks the whole range is going, if it hasn't actually gone, and of her extraordinary and unnatural activities, on her hands and knees, at half-past five in the morning.

I tell Cook—not without defiance—that A Man will come and look at the range whilst she is away. She says a *man* won't be able to do nothing. The Sweep, last time he saw it, said he couldn't understand how it was still holding together. In his opinion it wouldn't take more than a touch to send the whole thing to pieces, it was in such a way.

Sweep has evidently been very eloquent indeed, as Cook continues to quote him at immense length.

(*Note:* Make enquiries as to whether any other Sweep lives within a ten-mile radius, and if so, employ him for the future.)

Find myself edging nearer and nearer to the door, while at the same time continuing to look intelligently and responsively at Cook, but no break occurs in her discourse to enable me to disappear altogether.

After what seems like hours, Cook pauses for a moment and I again reiterate my intention of sending her for a holiday, to which she again replies that this is not necessary, nor even possible. Should like to ask whether Cook has ever heard of Mr. Bultitude who said that Everything would go to rack and ruin without him and was informed in return, not unreasonably, that he couldn't be as important as all that.

Instead, tell her that I shall expect her to be ready on Wednesday, and that Mrs. Vallence from the village is coming in to lend a hand.

Have just time to see, quite unwillingly, Cook assume an expression of horrified incredulity, before going out of the kitchen as quickly as I can.

Meet Aunt Blanche in the hall, and she asks if I am feeling ill as I am such a queer colour. Admit to feeling Upset, if not actually ill, after discussion in the kitchen and Aunt Blanche at once replies that she knows exactly what I mean, and it always does make a wreck of one, but I shall find that everything will go simply perfectly for at least a fortnight now. This is always the result of Speaking.

Feel that Aunt Blanche is right, and rally.

Serena very kindly takes the trouble to write and say that I am missed in the underworld,

that they have had another lecture on the treatment of shock, and everybody says the air-raids
are to begin on Sunday next. *P.S.:* She was
taken out to dinner last night by J. L. and
things are getting rather difficult, as she still
can't make up her mind. When I come back
she would like my advice.

(This leads to long train of thought as to the
advisability or otherwise of (*a*) asking and (*b*)
giving, advice. Reach the conclusion that both
are undesirable. Am convinced that nothing I
can say will in reality alter the course of Serena's existence, and that she probably knows
this as well as I do, but wants to talk to somebody. Can quite understand this, and am more
than ready to oblige her.)

Also receive official-looking envelope—no
stamp—and decide that the Ministry of Information has at last awakened to a sense of its
own folly in failing to utilise my services for the
nation, and has written to say so. Have already
mentally explained situation to Robert, left
Aunt Blanche to deal with Cook, packed up and
gone to London by 11.40—if still running—
before I have so much as slit open the envelope.

It turns out to be strongly-worded appeal on be-half of no-doubt excellent charity, in no way connected with the war.

Robert departs for his **A.R.P.**[1] office in small official two-seater, and tells me not to forget, if I want to take the car out, that I have barely three gallons of petrol and am not entitled to have my next supply until the twenty-third of the month.

I remind him in return about Mandeville Fitzwarren, and he assures me that he has not forgotten it at all and it's as safe as the Bank of England.

Go up and make the beds.

Doreen Fitzgerald, who is helping me, asserts that it is unlucky to turn the mattress on a Monday, and we accordingly leave it unturned. Learn subsequently from Aunt Blanche that D. F. holds similar views concerning Sundays, Fridays and the thirteenth of every month.

Learn from wireless News at one o'clock that Finnish-Soviet negotiations have been suspended, and am not in any way cheered by Aunt Blanche, who says that it is only a question of

[1] Air Raid Precautions.

[210]

time, now, before every country in Europe is dragged into war.

Lunch follows, and we make every effort not to talk of world situation in front of the children, but are only moderately successful, and Marigold—eating apple-tart—suddenly enquires in most intelligent tones whether I think the Germans will actually *land* in England, or only drop bombs on it from aeroplanes?

Instantly decide to take both Marigold and Margery out in car, petrol or no petrol, and have tea at small newly-opened establishment in neighbouring market town, by way of distracting their thoughts.

Both are upstairs, having official rest—(can hear Margery singing "South of the Border" very loudly and Marigold kicking the foot of the bed untiringly)—when Winnie opens drawing-room door and announces Lady B. with what seems like deliberate unexpectedness.

Lady B., whom I have not seen for months, has on admirable black two-piece garment, huge mink collar, perfectly brand-new pair of white gloves, exquisite shoes and stockings and tiny little black-white-red-blue-orange hat, intrinsically hideous but producing effect of extreme smartness and elegance.

Am instantly aware that my hair is out of curl, that I have not powdered my nose for hours, that my shoes—blue suède—bear no relation whatever to my dress—grey tweed—and that Aunt Blanche, who has said earlier in the day that she can't possibly go about for another minute in her old mauve wool cardigan, has continued to do so. Lady B. is doubtless as well aware as I am myself of these deficiencies, but both of us naturally ignore them, and assume appearance of delight in our reunion.

Aunt Blanche is introduced; Lady B. looks over the top of her head and says Don't let me disturb you, in very patronising tones indeed, and sits down without waiting to be asked.

What a world, she says, we're living in! All in it together. (Can see that this seems to her very odd.) We shall all alike suffer, all alike have to play our part—rich *and* poor.

Aunt Blanche, with great spirit, at once retorts that it won't be rich and poor at all, but poor and poor, with the new income-tax, and Lady B.—evidently a good deal startled—admits that Aunt Blanche is *too* right. She herself is seriously considering closing the London house, selling the villa in the South of France, making over the place in Scotland to the younger generation, and living quite, quite quietly on a crust in one half of the house at home.

Enquire whether she has taken any steps as yet towards accomplishing all this, and she says No, she is expecting a number of wounded officers at any moment, and has had to get the house ready for them. Besides, it would in any case be unpatriotic to dismiss members of the staff and cause unemployment, so Lady B. is keeping them all on except the second footman, who has been called up, and to whom she has said: Henry, you must *go*. The country has called for you, and I should be the very last person in the world not to wish you to go and fight. Leave your address and I will arrange to send you some cigarettes.

Henry, says Lady B., had tears in his eyes as he thanked her.

She then asks very solicitously what I have been doing to cause myself to look like a scarecrow, and she has heard that I am taking in evacuees, and where *have* I managed to squeeze them in, it's too clever of me for words.

Wonder whether to reply that I have set apart two *suites* for the evacuees and still have the whole of the West Wing empty, but decide on the truth as being simpler and more convincing, and merely inform Lady B. that as my own children are away, it is all very easy.

Lady B. at once supposes that My Girl, who must be quite grown-up by now, is working somewhere.

No, she's still at school, and will be for another two and a half years at least.

Lady B. says Really! in tones of astonishment. And what about My Boy? In France?

Not at all. In the Sixth at Rugby.

Ah, Rugby! says Lady B.

Am perfectly certain that in another second she is going to tell me about her nephews at Eton, and accordingly head her off by enquiring what she thinks about the probable duration of the war.

Lady B. shakes her head and is of opinion that we are not being told *everything*, by any means.

At the same time, she was at the War Office the other day (should like to know why, and how) and was told in strict confidence ——

At this point Lady B. looks round the room, as though expecting to see a number of the Gestapo hiding behind the curtains, and begs me to shut the window, if I don't mind. One never can be absolutely certain, and she has to be so particularly careful, because of being related to Lord Gort. (First I've ever heard of it.)

Shut the window—nothing to be seen outside except one blackbird on the lawn—and Aunt Blanche opens the door and then shuts it again.

Have often wondered what exact procedure would be if, on opening a door, Cook or Winnie should be discovered immediately outside it. Prefer not to pursue the thought.

Well, says Lady B., she knows that what she is going to say will *never* go beyond these four walls. At this she fixes her eyes on Aunt Blanche, who turns pale and murmurs Certainly not, and is evidently filled with apprehension.

Does Aunt Blanche, enquires Lady B., happen to know Violetta, Duchess of Tittington?

No.

Then do *I* know Violetta, Duchess of Titting-ton?

Am likewise obliged to disclaim Violetta, Duchess of Tittington—but dishonestly do so in rather considering tones, as though doubtful whether thinking of Violetta or of some other Duchess of my acquaintance.

Violetta, it seems, is a dear friend of Lady B.'s. She is naturally in close touch with the Cabinet, the House of Lords, the Speaker of the House of Commons, the War Office and Admiralty House. And from one or all of these sources, Violetta has deduced that a *lull* is expected shortly. It will last until the spring, and is all in favour of the Allies.

Will this lull, asks Aunt Blanche agitatedly, extend to the air? She is not, she adds hastily, in the least afraid of bombs or gas or anything of that kind—not at all—but it is very unsettling not to *know*. And, of course, we've all been expecting air-raids ever since the very beginning, and can't quite understand why they haven't happened.

Oh, they'll happen! declares Lady B. very authoritatively.

They'll *happen* all right—(surely rather curious form of qualification?)—and they'll be quite unpleasant. Aunt Blanche must be prepared for that. But at the same time she must remember that our defences are very good, and there's the balloon barrage to reckon with. The Duke, Violetta's husband, has pronounced that not more than one in fifteen of the enemy bombers will get through.

And will the raids all be over London? further enquires Aunt Blanche.

Try to convey to her in a single look that Lady B. is by no means infallible, and that I should be much obliged if Aunt Blanche wouldn't encourage her to believe that she is, and also that if we are to take evacuees out in the car, it is time this call came to an end—but message evidently beyond the compass of a single look, or of Aunt Blanche's powers of reception, and she continues to gaze earnestly at Lady B. through large pair of spectacles, reminding me of anxious, but intelligent, white owl.

Lady B. is grave, but not despairing, about London.

It will be the main objective, but a direct hit on any one particular building from the air is practically impossible. Aunt Blanche may take that as a fact.

Am instantly filled with a desire to repudiate it altogether, as a fact, and inform Lady B. that the river is unfortunately visible from the air at almost any height.

Completely defeated by Lady B., who adopts an attitude of deep concern and begs to be told instantly from what source I have heard this, as it is *exactly* the kind of inaccurate and mischievous rumour that the Government are most anxious to track down and expose.

As I have this moment evolved it, I find myself at a loss, and answer that I can't remember where I heard it.

I *must* remember, says Lady B. A great many utterly false statements of the kind are being circulated all over the country by Nazi propaganda agents, and the Authorities are determined to put an end to it. They are simply designed to impair the morale of the nation.

Can only assure her that I am practically certain it didn't emanate from a Nazi propaganda

[218]

agent—but Lady B. is still far from satisfied, and begs me to be very much more careful, and, above all, to communicate with her direct, the moment I meet with any kind of subversive rumour.

Should not dream of doing anything of the kind.

Aunt Blanche—do not care at all for the tone that she is taking—begs Lady B. for inside information in regard to the naval situation, and is told that this is Well in Hand. Lady B. was dining with the First Lord of the Admiralty only a few nights ago and he told her—but this must on no account go further—that the British Navy was doing wonders.

It always does, says Aunt Blanche firmly—at which she goes up in my estimation and I look at her approvingly, but she ignores me and continues to fix her eyes immovably on Lady B.

Tell myself, by no means for the first time, that Time and the Hour ride through the Roughest Day.

Lady B. asks what I have been doing in London and doesn't wait for an answer, but adds that she is very glad to see me back again,

[219]

as really there is plenty to do in one's own home nowadays, and no need to go out hunting for war jobs when there are plenty of *young* people ready and willing to undertake them.

Should like to inform Lady B. that I have been urgently invited to work for the Ministry of Information, but Aunt Blanche intervenes and states—intentions very kind but wish she had let it alone—that I am making myself *most* useful taking night duty at a W.V.S.[1] Canteen.

The one in Berkeley Square?

No, not the one in Berkeley Square. In the Adelphi.

Lady B. loses all interest on learning of this inferior locality, and takes her leave almost at once.

She looks round the study and tells me that I am quite right to have shut up the drawing-room—she herself is thinking of only using three or four of the downstairs rooms—and asks why I don't put down *parquet* flooring, as continual sweeping always does wear any carpet into holes, and professes to admire three very infe-

[1] Women's Voluntary Services.

[220]

rior chrysanthemums in pots, standing in the corner.

Do I know La Garonne? A lovely pink one, and always looks so well massed in the corners of a room or at the foot of the staircase.

(Should be very sorry to try to mass even two chrysanthemums in pots at the foot of my own staircase, as they would prevent anybody from either going up or down.)

Express civil interest in La Garonne and ring the bell for Winnie, who doesn't answer it. Have to escort Lady B. to hall door and waiting Bentley myself, and there bid her goodbye. Her last word is to the effect that if things get *too* difficult, am to ring her up as, in times like these, we must all do what we can for one another.

She then steps into Bentley, is respectfully shrouded in large fur rug by chauffeur, and driven away.

Return to study fire and inform Aunt Blanche that, much as I dislike everything I have ever heard or read about Stalin and his régime, there are times when I should feel quite prepared to join Communist party. Aunt Blanche only answers, with great common sense, that she does not think I had better say anything of that kind in front of Robert, and what about telling Marigold and Margery to get ready for their drive?

Follow her advice and very successful expedition ensues, with much running downhill with car in neutral gear, in the hope that this saves petrol, and tea at rather affected little hostelry recently opened under the name of Betty's Buttery.

Return before black-out and listen to the Six O'clock News. German aircraft have made daylight raid over Firth of Forth and have been driven off, and aerial battle has been watched from the streets by the inhabitants of Edinburgh.

Aunt Blanche waxes very indignant over this, saying that her sister-in-law *deliberately* went up North in search of safety and now she has had all this excitement and seen the whole thing. She is unable to get over this for the rest of the evening, and says angrily at intervals that it's all so exactly *like* Eleanor.

Evening passes uneventfully. Robert returns, says that he's already heard the News, seems

Do I know La Garonne?

unwilling to enter into any discussion of it, and immerses himself in *Times* crossword puzzle. Aunt Blanche not deterred by this from telling him all about air-raid over Firth of Forth with special emphasis on the fact of her sister-in-law Eleanor having been there and, as she rather strangely expresses it, had all the fun for nothing.

Robert makes indeterminate sound, but utters no definite comment.

Later on, however, he suggests that Vicky's school, on the East Coast, may have heard something of raid and that, if so, she will be delighted.

October 18th.—Long letter from Vicky informs us that school *did* receive air-raid warning, interrupting a lacrosse match, and that everybody had to go into the shelter. The weather has been foul, and a most divine concert has taken place, with a divine man playing the violin marvellously. Vicky is trying a new way of doing her hair, curled under, and some of her friends say it's like Elizabeth Bergner and others say it's simply frightful. Tons of love and Vicky is frightfully sorry for sending such a deadly letter but it's been a frightfully dull term and nothing ever seems to happen.

Robert, at this, enquires caustically what the young want nowadays? Nothing ever satisfies them.

October 19th.—Cook steeped in gloom, is driven by myself to distant cross-roads where she is met by an uncle, driving a large car full of milk-cans. Her suitcase is wedged amongst the milk-cans, and she tells me in sepulchral tones that if she's wanted back in a hurry I can always ring up the next farm—name of Blore— and they'll always run across with a message and she can be got as far as the cross-roads if not all the way, as uncle has plenty of petrol.

Take my leave of her, reflecting how much more fortunately situated uncle is than I am myself.

Mrs. Vallence is in the kitchen on my return and instantly informs me that she isn't going to say a word. Not a single word. But it'll take her all her time, and a bit over, just to get things cleaned up.

I give a fresh turn to the conversation by suggesting that I am anxious to learn as much as

I can in the way of cooking, and should be glad
of anything that Mrs. Vallence can teach me,
and we come to an amicable agreement regarding my presence in the kitchen at stated hours
of the day.

Indulge in long and quite unprofitable fan-
tasy of myself preparing and cooking very superior meals for (equally superior) succession
of Paying Guests, at the end of the war. Just as
I have achieved a really remarkable dinner
of which the principal features are lobster
a l'Américaine and grapes in spun sugar, Winnie comes in to say that the grocer has called for
orders please'm and Mrs. Vallence says to say
that we're all right except for a packet of cornflour and half-a-dozen of eggs for the cakes if
that'll be all right.

I give my sanction to the packet of cornflour
and half-dozen of eggs and remind myself that
there is indeed a wide difference between fact
and fancy.

This borne in on me even more sharply at a
later hour when Mrs. Vallence informs me that
gardener has sent in two lovely rabbits and
they'll come in handy for to-morrow's lunch

and give me an opportunity of seeing how they ought to be got ready, which is a thing many ladies never have any idea of whatever.

Do not care to reply that I should be more than content to remain with the majority in this respect.

October 21st.—Aunt Blanche tells me very seriously to have nothing to do with rabbits. Breakfast scones if I like, mayonnaise sauce and an occasional sweet if I really feel I must, but *not* rabbits. They can, and should, be left to professional cooks.

Could say a great deal in reply, to the effect that professional cooks are anything but numerous and that those there are will very shortly be beyond my means—but remember in time that argument with the elderly, more especially when a relative, is of little avail and go to the kitchen without further discussion.

Quite soon afterwards am wishing from the bottom of my heart that I had taken Aunt Blanche's advice.

This gives place, after gory and unpleasant interlude, to rather more self-respecting frame of mind, and Mrs. V. tells me approvingly that I have now done The Worst Job in all Cooking.

Am thankful to hear it.

Rabbit-stew a success, but make my own lunch off scrambled eggs.

October 24th.—Obliged to ring up Cook's uncle's neighbour and ask him to convey a message to the effect that petrol will be insufficient to enable me to go and meet her either at station or bus stop. Can the uncle convey her to the door, or must conveyance be hired?

Aunt Blanche says that Robert has plenty of A.R.P.[1] petrol, she supposes, but Robert frowns severely on this, and says with austerity that he hasn't plenty at all—only just enough to enable him to perform his duties.

Aunt Blanche inclined to be hurt at Robert's tone of voice and, quite unjustly, becomes hurt with me as well, and when I protest says that she doesn't know what I mean, there's nothing the matter at all, and she's not the kind of person to take offence at nothing, and never has been. I ought to know her better than that, after all these years.

Assure her in return that of course I do, but this not a success either and I go off to discuss Irish stew and boiled apple pudding with Mrs.

[1] Air Raid Precautions.

Vallence in kitchen, leaving Aunt Blanche looking injured over the laundry book. She is no
better when I return, and tells me that practically not a single table napkin is fit to be seen
and most of them are One Large Darn.

Receive distinct impression that Aunt
Blanche feels that I am solely to blame for this,
and cannot altogether escape uneasy feeling that
perhaps I am.

(*Query:* Why? Is not this distressing example of suggestibility amounting to weak-
mindedness? *Answer:* Do not care to contemplate it.)

Can see that it will be useless to ask Aunt
Blanche if she would like to accompany me to
village, and accordingly go there without her
but with Marigold dashing ahead on Fairy
bicycle and Margery pedalling very slowly on
minute tricycle.

Expedition fraught with difficulty owing to
anxiety about Marigold, always just ahead of
me whisking round corners from which I feel
certain that farm lorry is about to appear, and
necessity of keeping an eye on Margery, continually dropping behind and evidently in ut-

most distress every time the lane slopes either up or down. Suggestion that she might like to push tricycle for a bit only meets with head-shakes accompanied by heavy breathing.

Am relieved and astonished when village is achieved without calamity and bicycle and tricycle are left outside Post-Office whilst M. and M. watch large, mottled-looking horse being shod at the forge.

Mrs. S. at the Post-Office—having evidently been glued to the window before recalled to the counter—observes that they look just like Princess Elizabeth and Princess Margaret, don't they?

Can see no resemblance whatever, but reply amiably and untruthfully that perhaps they do, a little.

Long and enthralling conversation ensues, in the course of which I learn that Our Vicar's Wife has Got Help at last—which sounds spiritual, but really means that she has found A Girl from neighbouring parish who isn't, according to Mrs. S., not anyways what you'd called trained, but is thought not to mind being *told*. We agree that this is better than nothing, and

Mrs. S. adds darkly that we shall be seeing a bit of a change in the Girls, unless she's very much mistaken, with the gentry shutting up their houses all over the place, like, and there's a many Girls will find out that they didn't know which way their bread was buttered, before so very long.

I point out in return that nobody's bread is likely to be buttered at all, once rationing begins, and Mrs. S. appears delighted with this witticism and laughs heartily. She adds encouragingly that Marge is now a very different thing from what it was in the last war.

Hope with all my heart that she may be right.

A three-shilling book of stamps, then says Mrs. S.—making no effort to produce it—and can I tell her what Russia is going to do?

No, not definitely at the moment.

Well, says Mrs. S., Hitler, if he'd asked *her*, wouldn't never have got himself into this mess. For it *is* a mess, and if he doesn't know it now, he soon will.

Can see that if Mrs. S. and I are to cover the whole range of European politics it will take most of the day, and again recall her to my requirements.

We discuss the Women's Institute—speakers very difficult to get, and Mrs. S. utterly scouts my suggestion that members should try and entertain one another, asserting that none of our members would care to put themselves forward, she's quite sure, and there'd only be remarks passed if they did—and rumour to the effect that a neighbouring Village Hall has been Taken Away from the W.I. by the A.R.P.[1] The W.I. has pleaded to be allowed to hold its Monthly Meetings there and has finally been told that it may do so, on the sole condition that in the event of an air-raid alarm the members will instantly all vacate the Hall and go out into the street.

It is not known whether conditions have been agreed to or not, but Mrs. S. would like to know if I can tell her, once and for all, whether we are to expect any air-raids or not, and if so, will they be likely to come over the Village?

Can only say to this that I Hope Not, and again ask for stamps which Mrs. S. produces from a drawer, and tells me that she's sorry for Finland and is afraid they're in for trouble and that'll be three shillings.

[1] Air Raid Precautions.

Horse at the forge still being shod, and evacuees Marigold and Margery still rooted to the ground looking at it. Am about to join them when smart blow on the shoulder causes me to turn round, very angry, and confront Miss Pankerton.

Miss P. is in khaki—cannot imagine any colour less suited to her—and looks very martial indeed except for pince-nez, quite out-of-place but no doubt inevitable.

She has come to meet her six young toughs, she says, now due out of school. Regular East End scallywags, they are, but Miss P. has made them toe the line and has no trouble with them now. I shall see in a few minutes.

And what, asks Miss P., am I doing? A woman of my intelligence ought to be at the very heart of things at a time like this.

Fleeting, but extraordinarily powerful, feeling comes over me that I have often thought this myself, but that this does not in any way interfere with instant desire to contradict Miss P. flatly.

Compromise—as usual—by telling her that I am not really doing very much, I have two very nice evacuated children and their nurse in the house and am a good deal in London, where I work at a Canteen.

But, replies Miss P.—in voice that cannot fail to reach Mrs. S. again at Post-Office window, which she has now opened—but this is pure *Nonsense*. I ought to be doing something of *real* importance. One of the very first things she thought of, when war broke out, was me. Now, she said to herself, that unfortunate woman will have her chance at last. She can stop frittering her time and her talents away, and Find Herself at last. It is *not*, whatever I may say, too late.

Can only gaze at Miss Pankerton with horror, but she quite misunderstands the look and begs me, most energetically, to pull myself together at once. Whitehall is Crying Out for executives.

I inform Miss P. that if so, cries have entirely failed to reach me, or anybody else that I've met. On the contrary, everybody is asking to be given a job and nobody is getting one.

I have, says Miss P., gone to the wrong people.

No, I reply, I haven't.

[233]

Deadlock has evidently been reached and Miss P. and I glare at one another in the middle of the street, no doubt affording interesting material for conjecture to large number of our neighbours.

Situation is relieved by general influx of children coming out of school. Miss P.'s toughs materialise and turn out to be six pallid and undersized little boys, all apparently well under nine years old.

Am rather relieved to see that they look cheerful, and not as though bullied by Miss P., who presently marshals them all into a procession and walks off with them.

Parting observation to me is a suggestion that I ought to join the W.A.A.F.[1] and that Miss P. could probably arrange it for me, at which I thank her coldly and say I shouldn't think of such a thing. Miss P.—quite undaunted—calls back over her shoulder that perhaps I'm right, it isn't altogether in my line, and I'd better go to the Ministry of Information, they've got a scheme for making use of the Intellectuals.

[1] Women's Auxiliary Air Force.

Should like to yell back in reply that I am not an Intellectual and don't wish to be thought one—but this proceeding undignified, and moreover only very powerful screech indeed could reach Miss Pankerton, now half-way up the hill, with toughs capering along beside her looking like so many white mice.

Turn to collect Marigold and Margery—both have disappeared and are subsequently retrieved from perfectly harmless-seeming lane from which they have mysteriously collected tar all over their shoes.

Make every effort to remove this with handfuls of grass—have no expectations of succeeding, nor do I—and say It's lucky it didn't get onto their coats, and proceed homewards. Find tar on both coats on arriving, also on Marigold's jumper and Margery's socks.

Apologise to Doreen Fitzgerald, tell her I'm afraid she may find it rather difficult to remove, and she answers bitterly Certainly I will, and I feel that relations between us have not been improved.

Situation with regard to Aunt Blanche is fortunately easier and at lunch we talk quite pleasantly about Serena—whom Aunt Blanche still refers to as Serena Fiddlededee—and National Registration Cards.

Do I know, enquires Aunt Blanche, that if one loses one's Identity Card, one is issued with a *bright scarlet* one?

Like the Scarlet Woman? I ask.

Yes, exactly like that, or else the Scarlet Letter—Aunt Blanche isn't sure which, or whether both are the same, but anyway it's a scarlet card, and even if lost Identity Card reappears, the scarlet one cannot be replaced, but remains forever.

Can only reply, after a long silence, that it sounds perfectly terrible, and Aunt Blanche says Oh yes, it is.

Conversation only revives when infant Margery abruptly informs us that she made two of the beds unaided this morning.

Commend her highly for this and she looks gratified, but have inward misgiving that her parents, if they hear of her domestic activities, may think that I have made her into a household drudge.

Offer her and Marigold the use of gramophone and all the records for the whole afternoon.

Aunt Blanche, later, tells me that she does not think this was at all a good idea.

Second post brings me letter from Serena. I am much missed at the Canteen, and Mrs. Peacock has said that mine is a *bright* face, and she hopes soon to see it back again. (Serena, to this, adds three exclamation marks—whether denoting admiration or astonishment, am by no means certain. Do not, in any case, care for Mrs. P.'s choice of descriptive adjective.)

The underworld, Serena informs me, is a seething mass of intrigue and Darling and the Commandant have made up their quarrel and are never out of one another's pockets for a single instant, but on the other hand Mrs. Nettleship (First Aid) and Miss Carloe-Hill (Ambulance Driver) have had the most tremendous row and are not speaking to one another, and everybody is taking sides and threatening to resign as a protest.

Serena herself hasn't slept for nights and nights because there's been a ping-pong craze and people play it all night long, just outside the Rest-room, and J. L. has taken her out to dinner and to a dreadful film, all full of Nazi atrocities, and this has ensured still further wakefulness.

Serena ends by begging me in most affectionate terms to come back, as she misses me dreadfully, and it's all awful. Have I read a book called *The Confidential Agent*? It's fearfully good, but dreadfully upsetting, and perhaps I'd better not.

(If *The Confidential Agent* had not been on my library list already—which it is—should instantly have put it there.)

Am asked by Aunt Blanche, rather apologetically, if that is a letter from Serena Fiddle-dedee? She didn't, needless to say, *look* at the envelope, nor has she, of course, the slightest wish to know anything about my private correspondence—but she couldn't help *seeing* that I had a letter from Serena.

Have too often said exactly the same thing myself to entertain the slightest doubt as to Aunt Blanche's veracity, and offer to show her Serena's letter at once as there is nothing private about it.

[238]

No, no, she didn't mean that, Aunt Blanche assures me—at the same time putting on her spectacles with one hand and taking the letter with the other. When she comes to J. L. Aunt Blanche emits rather inarticulate exclamation and at once enquires if I don't think it would be a very good thing?

Well, no, on the whole I don't. It doesn't seem to me that Serena cares two straws about him.

Aunt Blanche moans, and says it seems a very great pity, then cheers up again and declares that when J. L. gets into uniform and is sent out to fight, it will probably make all the difference, and Serena will find out that she *does* care about him, and one can only hope it won't then be too late.

Perceive that Aunt Blanche and I hold fundamentally divergent views on what does or does not constitute a successful love-affair, and abandon the topic.

Evening closes in with return of Cook, who looks restored and tells me that she enjoyed her holiday and spent most of it in helping her uncle's second wife to make marrow jam.

[239]

Enquire of Robert whether he thinks he can spare me if I return to London on Thursday.

He replies that he supposes he can, and asks what I think I shall do, up there?

Write articles about London in Wartime, I suggest, and help at W.V.S.[1] Canteen. Should like to add, Get Important job at Ministry of Information—but recollections of Miss Pankerton forbid.

Robert seems unenthusiastic, but agrees that he is not likely to be much at home and that Aunt Blanche can manage the house all right. He incomprehensibly adds: Who is this Birdie that she is always talking about?

Can only enquire in return: What birdie?

Some name of that kind, Robert says. And a double-barrelled surname. Not unlike Gammon-and-Spinach, and yet *not* quite that. Instantly recognise old Granny Bo-Peep and suggest that he means Pussy Winter-Gammon, to which Robert replies Yes, that's what he said, isn't it.

Explain old Mrs. W.-G. to him in full and Robert, after a long silence, remarks that it

[1] Women's Voluntary Services.

[240]

sounds to him as though what she needed was the lethal chamber.

October 26th.—Robert leaves me at the station on his way to A.R.P.[1] office, with parting information that he thinks—he is not certain at all but he *thinks*—that the gas-masks for the inhabitants of Mandeville Fitzwarren are now available for distribution.

Train comes in late, and is very crowded. Take up commanding position at extreme edge of platform and decide to remain there firmly and on no account join travellers hurrying madly from one end of train to the other. Am obliged to revise entire scheme of action when I find myself opposite coach consisting entirely of first-class carriages. Third-class, by the time I reach it, completely filled by other people and their luggage. Get in as best I can and am looked at with resentment amounting to hatred by four strangers already comfortably installed in corner seats.

Retire at once behind illustrated daily paper and absorb stream of Inside Information from column which I now regard as being practically

[1] Air Raid Precautions.

omniscient. Can only suppose that its special correspondent spends his days and nights concealed in, alternately, Hitler's waste-paper basket and Stalin's ink-pot.

Realise too late that I have placed bag in rack, sandwiched amongst much other luggage, and that it contains library book on which I am relying to pass the journey.

Shall be more unpopular than ever if I now get up and try to disentangle bag.

Postpone things as long as possible by reading illustrated paper all over again, and also printed notice—inconsiderately pasted over looking-glass—telling me how I am to conduct myself in the event of an air-raid.

Suggestion that we should all lie down on floor of the carriage rouses in me no enthusiasm, and I look at all my fellow travellers in turn and, if possible, care about the idea even less than before.

Following on this I urge myself to Make an Effort, Mrs. Dombey, and actually do so, to the extent of getting up and attacking suitcase. Prolonged struggle results in, no doubt, fearful though unseen havoc amongst folded articles in case and extraction of long novel about Victorian England.

Sit down again feeling, and doubtless looking, as though all my clothes had been twisted round back to front, and find that somebody has opened a window with the result that several pieces of my hair blow intermittently into my eyes and over my nose.

This happens to nobody else in the carriage.

Am not in the least interested by long novel about Victorian England and think the author would have known more about it after a course of Charlotte M. Yonge. Sleep supervenes and am awakened by complete stranger patting me sharply on the knee and asking Do I want Reading?

No, it is very kind of her, but I do not.

Complete stranger gets out and I take the occasion of replacing book in suitcase and observing in pocket-mirror that sleep, theoretically so beneficial, has appalling effect on the appearance of anybody over thirty years of age.

Do my best to repair its ravages.

Reappearance of fellow traveller, carrying cup of tea, reminds me that luncheon car is no longer available and I effect purchase of ham roll through the window.

Step back again into cup of tea, which has been idiotically placed on the floor.

Apologies naturally ensue. I blame myself entirely and say that I am dreadfully sorry—which indeed I am—unknown lady declares heroically that it doesn't really matter, she'd had all she wanted (this can't possibly be true) —and I tell her that I will get her another cup of tea.

No, really.

Yes, yes, I insist.

Train starts just as she makes up her mind to accept, and I spend remainder of the journey thinking remorsefully how thirsty she must be.

We exchange no further words, but part at Paddington, where I murmur wholly inarticulate farewell and she smiles at me reproachfully in return.

Flat has been adorned with flowers, presumably by Serena, and this makes up for revolting little pile of correspondence, consisting entirely of very small bills, uninteresting advertisements, and circular letters asking me to subscribe to numerous deserving causes.

Spend entire evening in doing, so far as I can see, nothing in particular and eventually ring up Rose to see if she has got a job yet.

Am not in the least surprised to hear that she hasn't.

She says that if it wasn't for the black-out she would invite me to come and have supper with her, and I reply that if it wasn't for the black-out I should simply love to come. This seems to be as near as we get to any immediate rendezvous, and I ring off rather dejectedly.

Go out to Chinese basement restaurant across the street and restore my morale with exotic dish composed of rice, onions and unidentifiable odds and ends.

October 29th.—Have occasion to remark, as often before in life, that quite a short absence from any given activity almost invariably results in finding it all quite different on return. Canteen no exception to this rule.

Mrs. Peacock has completely disappeared—nothing to do with leg, which I fear at first may have taken a turn for the worse—and is said to have transferred her services to another branch —professional cashier has taken over cash-register and sits entrenched with it behind a

high wooden barricade as though expecting rob-
bery with violence at any minute—and two
enormous new urns are installed at one end of
counter, rather disquietingly labelled Danger.
Enquire humorously of lady in charge whether
they are filled with explosives and she looks
perfectly blank and replies in a strong Scottish
accent that One wad be the hot milk like, and
the other the coffee.

Serena is not on duty when I arrive, and tele-
phone-call to her flat has only produced very
long and painstaking statement in indifferent
English from one of her Refugees, of which I
understand scarcely a word, except that Serena
is The Angel of Hampstead, is it not? Agree
that it is, and exchange cordial farewells with
the Refugee who says something that I think
refers to the goodness of my heart. (Unde-
served.)

Canteen gramophone has altered its repertoire
—this a distinct relief—and now we have "Love
Never Grows Old" and "Run, rabbit, run."
Final chorus to the latter—Run, Hitler, run—I
think a great mistake and quote to myself Dr.
Dunstan from *The Human Boy*: "It ill becomes

us, sir, to jest at a fallen potentate—and still less before he has fallen."

Helpers behind the counter now number two very young and rather pretty sisters, who say that they wish to be called Patricia and Juanita. Tendency on the part of all the male *clientèle* to be served by them and nobody else, and they hold immense conversations, in undertones, with youths in leather jackets and brightly-coloured ties.

This leaves Red Cross workers, female ambulance drivers, elderly special constables and stretcher-bearers, to me.

One of these—grey-headed man in spectacles—comes up and scrutinises the menu at great length and then enquires What there is, to-night? Suppose his sight has been dimmed by time, and offer to read him the list. He looks offended and says No, no, he has read it. Retrieve this error by asserting that I only made the suggestion because the menu seemed to be so illegibly written.

Instant judgment follows, as Scottish lady leans down from elevation beside the urns and says severely that *she* wrote out those cards and took particular pains to see that they were *not* illegible.

Decide to abandon the whole question without attempting any explanations whatever.

Brisk interlude follows, time goes by before I know it, and at eleven o'clock Serena suddenly materialises and asks for coffee—as usual—and says that she is so glad I've come back. Can't I take my supper now and come and join her?

Yes, I can. Am entitled to free meal and, after much consideration, select sardines, bread-and-butter, tea and two buns. Inform Serena, on principle, that I do not approve of feminine habit of eating unsuitable food at unseasonable hours whilst working, and that I had a proper dinner before I came out.

Serena begs me not to be so grown-up and asks what the meal was. Am obliged to turn the conversation rather quickly, as have just remembered that it was taken in a hurry at a milk-bar and consisted of soup and tinned-salmon sandwich.

What, I ask, has Serena been doing?

Serena groans and says Oh, on Sunday morn-

ing there was an air-raid alarm and she was all
ready for anything, and started up her car, and
then the whole thing petered out. She popped
up into the street and saw the Embankment Gardens balloon getting ready to defend England,
but as soon as the All Clear was given, it came
down again, which Serena thinks denotes slack-
ness on the part of somebody.

She has also been seeing J. L. and would
like to talk to me some time, and could she
bring him to the flat for a drink one evening?

Yes, certainly—to-morrow if she likes.

Serena sighs, and looks distressed, and says
That would be great fun. J. L. wants cheer-
ing-up—in fact, he's utterly wretched. He has
finished his novel, and it is all about a woman
whose husband is a political prisoner in a Concentration Camp and she can't get news of him
and she goes on the streets and one of her children is an epileptic and the other one joins a
gang and goes to the bad, and in the end this
woman gets shot and the children are just left
starving in a cellar. J. L. thinks that it is the
very best piece of work he's ever done, and his
publishers say Yes, it is, but they don't feel

sure that anybody is going to want to read it just now, let alone buy it.

They have gone so far as to suggest that what people want is something more like P. G. Wodehouse, and J. L. is greatly upset, not because he does not admire P. G. Wodehouse, but because he feels himself to be so entirely incapable of emulating him.

Serena, rather fortunately, does not enquire whether my views on topical fiction coincide with those of J. L. or those of his publishers, and we proceed to the discussion of wider issues.

What does Serena think of the news?

Well, she doesn't think we're being *told* much. It's all very well to say our aircraft is always flying about all over Germany and the Siegfried Line, but do we really *always* return intact without a single casualty? Nor does she understand about Russia.

Russia, according to the news, can't do anything at all. They have masses of oil and masses of grain and probably masses of ammunition as well, but no Russian transport is apparently capable of moving a yard without instantly

breaking down, all Russian ports are stiff with
ice throughout three-quarters of the year, and
no Russian engineers, telephone-operators,
engine-drivers, miners or business executives
are able at any time to take any constructive
action whatsoever.

Serena cannot help feeling that if Russia had
signed a pact with us, instead of with Germany,
this would all be described quite differently.

She also complains that Nazi aircraft has so
far directed all its activities towards the North.
Scotland, in the opinion of Serena, always has
been rather inclined to think itself the hub of
the universe, and this will absolutely clinch it.
The Scots will now suppose that the enemy
share their own opinion, that Edinburgh is more
important than London.

As for the Ministry of Information, Serena
is *sorry* for it. Definitely and absolutely sorry.
Look at the things that people have said about
it in Parliament, and outside Parliament for
that matter, and all the things in the papers!
They may have made their mistakes, Serena
admits, but the really fatal blunder was to call
them Ministry of Information in a war where

[251]

the one thing that nobody is allowed to have is any information.

Have they, she adds, done anything about me yet?

Nothing whatever.

I am proposing to go there, however, on the strength of a letter of introduction from Uncle A. who stood godfather, some thirty years ago, to the Head of one of the Departments.

He is not, as yet, aware of the privilege in store for him.

Serena hopes that I shall be able to find him, but has heard that the Ministry—situated in London University buildings—is much larger than the British Museum and far less well sign-posted. Moreover, if one asks for anybody, one is always told, firstly, that he has never been there at all; secondly, that he isn't in the department over which he is supposed to be reigning; thirdly, that the department itself is not to be found because it has moved to quite another part of the building and nobody knows where it is, and fourthly, that he left the Ministry altogether ten days ago.

Can quite see that I shall be well advised to allow plenty of time for the projected visit.

Serena's fellow worker, Muriel, appears and asks whether we have heard that the Ritz Hotel has out-distanced all other hotels, which merely advertise Air-Raid Shelter, by featuring elegant announcement outside its portals: *Abri du Ritz.*

Shall look at it next time I am waiting for a bus in Piccadilly, which is the only occasion on which I am in the least likely to find myself even outside entrance to the Ritz, let alone inside it.

Finish supper and return to my own side of the counter.

Inhabitants of the underworld invariably take on second lease of life towards midnight, and come in search of eggs and bacon—bacon now Off; shepherd's pie all finished; and toad-in-the-hole just crossed off the list. Do the best we can with scrambled eggs, sausages and ham —which also runs low before the night is out.

Scottish tea-dispenser presently gets down from high seat which enables her to deal with urns, and commands, rather than requests me, to take her place.

Do so quite successfully for an hour, when hot-milk tap, for no reason known to me, turns on but declines to turn off and floods the floor, also my own shoes and stockings.

Succeed in turning it off again after some damage and much expenditure of milk.

Professional cashier says Dear, dear, it does seem a waste of milk, doesn't it? and Patricia suggests without enthusiasm that it really ought to be mopped up.

Am in full agreement with both, but feel unreasonably annoyed with them and go home, after mopping-up, inclined to tell myself that I have evidently outlived such powers of usefulness as were ever mine. This conviction continues during process of undressing and increases by leaps and bounds when bath-water turns out cold.

(*Note:* Minor calamities of life apt to assume importance in inverse ratio to advancing hours of the night. *Query:* Will the black-out in any way affect this state of affairs?)

Kettle in no hurry to boil water for bottle, and go to bed eventually feeling chilly and dejected.

October 31st.—Visit the Ministry of Information and find vast area of Hall, where I am eyed with disfavour by Minor Official in uniform who wishes to know what I want.

I want Mr. Molesworth, and have had enough presence of mind to arrange appointment with him by telephone.

Minor Official repeats *Molesworth?* in tones of utter incredulity, and fantastic wonder crosses my mind as to what he would say if I suddenly replied, Oh no, I didn't mean Molesworth at all. I just said that for fun. What I *really* meant all the time was Fisher.

Realise instantly that this would serve no good purpose, and reiterate Molesworth. At this Minor Official shakes his head very slowly, looks at a book, and shakes his head again.

But I have, I urge, an appointment.

This evidently necessitates calling in a second opinion, and somebody standing by a lift is asked if he knows anything about Molesworth.

Molesworth? No. Wait a minute. *Molesworth?* Yes.

Where can he be found?

Second Opinion hasn't the least idea. He *was* up on the sixth floor, last week, but that's all been changed now. Miss Hogg may know.

[255]

Miss Hogg—evidently less elusive than some of her collaborators—is telephoned to. Reply, received after a long wait, is inaudible to me but Minor Official reports that I had better try the third floor; he can't say for certain, but Mr. M. *was* there at one time, and Miss Hoggs hasn't heard of his having moved.

Start off hopefully for lift, am directed to go right across the hall and into quite another part of the building, and take the lift there. Final inspiration of Minor Official is to ask whether I know the number of Mr. M.'s Room —which of course I don't.

Walk along lengthy passages for what seems like some time, and meet with kindness, but no definite information, from several blonde young lovelies who mostly—rather mistakenly —favour scarlet jumpers.

Compare myself mentally with Saracen lady, said to have travelled to England in search of her lover with no vocabulary except two words, *London* and *Gilbert*. (London in those days probably much smaller than Ministry of Information in these.)

Astonishment temporarily surpasses relief

[256]

Molesworth?

when I am at last definitely instructed by young
red-headed thing—fortunately *not* in scarlet—
to Room 568. Safeguards herself by adding
that Mr. M. *was* there an hour ago, but of
course he may have been moved since then.

He hasn't.

His name is on a card over the door.

Shall be surprised if I do not hear myself
calling him Gilbert.

Am horrified to find myself quarter of an
hour after appointed time, and feel it is only
what I deserve when Mr. M. keeps me waiting
for twenty minutes.

Eventually meet him face to face across his
own writing-table and he is kindness and civility
personified, tells me that he hasn't seen Uncle
A. since early childhood but still has silver
mug bestowed at his christening, and has always
heard that the old gentleman is wonderful.

Yes indeed. Wonderful.

Cannot avoid the conclusion that contemplat-
ing the wonderfulness of Uncle A. will get us
no further in regard to winning the war, and
suggest, I hope diffidently, that I should much
like to do something in this direction.

Mr. M. tells me that *this* war is quite unlike that of 1914. (Not where Ministries are concerned it isn't—but do not tell him this.)

In 1914, he says instructively, a tremendous Machinery had to be set in motion, and this was done with the help of unlimited expenditure and numerous experiments. *This* time it is all different. The Machinery is expected to be, at the very beginning, all that it was at the very end last time. And expenditure is not unlimited at all. Far from it.

I say No, I suppose not—as though having given the question a good deal of thought.

Mr. M. then successively talks about the French, the Turks, the Russians, and recent reconnaissance flights over Germany.

I suggest that I mustn't take up any more of his time. I really only wanted to see if I could do some kind of work.

He appreciates my offer, replies Mr. M., and tells me about Hore-Belisha and the House of Commons.

I offer him in return my opinion of Winston Churchill—favourable—and of Sir Samuel Hoare—not so good.

[258]

We find ourselves—I cannot say how—talking of the self-government of India.

A man with a beard and an appearance of exhaustion comes in, apologises, is begged not to go away, and we are introduced—his name inaudible to me, as doubtless mine to him.

He tells me almost at once that *this* war is quite unlike that of 1914. Tremendous machinery set in motion . . . expenditure . . . experiment. . . . *This* time, Machinery expected to begin at stage previously reached in 1918. . . .

Try to look as though I haven't heard all this before, express concern at state of affairs depicted, and explain that I am anxious to place my services—etc.

Ah, says the beard, it is being found very difficult—very, very difficult indeed—to make use of all those whom the Ministry would *like* to make use of. Later on, no doubt, the right field of activity will present itself—much, much later on.

Does he, then, think that the war is going to be a lengthy affair?

It would, says Mr. M. gravely, be merely

[259]

wishful thinking to take too optimistic a view. The probabilities are that nothing much will happen for some months—perhaps even longer. But let us not look further ahead than the winter.

The long, cold, dark, dreary, interminable winter lies ahead of us—petrol will be less, travelling more restricted, the black-out more complete and the shortage of certain foodstuffs more noticeable. People will be *tired* of the war. Their morale will tend to sink lower and lower.

Quote to myself:

> The North wind doth blow
> And we shall have snow,
> And what will Robin do then, poor thing?

but feel that it would be quite out of place to say this aloud.

I ask instead whether there is anything I can do, to alleviate the melancholy state of things that evidently lies ahead.

All of us can do something, replies Mr. M. There are, for instance, a number of quite false rumours going about. These can be tracked to their source—(how?)—discredited and contradicted.

The man with the beard breaks in, to tell me that in the last war there were innumerable alarms concerning spies in our midst.

(As it is quite evident, notwithstanding the beard, that he was still in his cradle at the time of the last war, whilst I had left mine some twenty years earlier, this information would really come better from me to him.)

The Government wishes to sift these rumours, one and all—(they will have their hands full if they undertake anything of the kind)—and it is possible to assist them in this respect. Could I, for instance, tell him what is being said in the extreme North of England where I live?

Actually, it is in the extreme *West* that I live.

Of course, of course. Mr. M. knew it perfectly well—nothing he knows better—extraordinary slip of the tongue only. What exactly, then, is being said in the extreme West?

Complete blank comes over me. Can remember nothing but that we have all told ourselves that even if butter *is* rationed we can get plenty of clotted cream, and that we really needn't bother to take our gas-masks wherever we go.

Can only summon to my help very feeble statement to the effect that our morale seems to be in very good repair and that our evacuees seem to be settling down—at which he looks disappointed, as well he may.

Can see that my chances of getting a job— never very good—are now practically moribund.

Raise the subject again, although not confidently, and Mr. M. tells me—evidently in order to get rid of me—that I had better see Captain Skein-Tring. He is—or *was*, two days ago—in Room 4978, on the fourth floor, in the other building. Do I think I can find my way there?

Know perfectly well that I can't, and say so frankly, and Mr. M. sighs but handsomely offers to escort me himself, and does so.

On the way, we talk about the Papal Encyclical, Uncle A. again, and the B.B.C.[1] Mr. M.

[1] British Broadcasting Corporation.

is pained about most of the programmes and thinks they are too *bright* and why so much cinema organ? I defend the B.B.C. and tell him I like most of the popular music, but not the talks to housewives.

Mr. M. sighs heavily and no point of agreement is found, until we find a joint admiration for L. A. G. Strong's short stories.

Just as this desirable stage is reached, we meet with a pallid young man carrying hundreds of files, to whom Mr. M. says compassionately, Hallo, Basil, moving again?

Basil says Yes, wearily, and toils on, and Mr. M. explains that Poor Basil has been moved three times within the last ten days.

Just as he disappears from view Mr. M. recalls him, to ask if he knows whether Captain Skein-Tring is still in Propaganda, 4978. Basil looks utterly bewildered and replies that he has never heard of anybody called Skein-Tring. Anyhow, the Propaganda people have all been transferred now, and the department has been taken over by the people from National Economy.

Mr. M. groans, but pushes valiantly on, and

[263]

this bulldog spirit is rewarded by totally unexpected appearance—evidently the very last thing he has expected—of Captain S.-T.'s name on the door of Room 4978. He accordingly takes me in and introduces me, assures me that I shall be absolutely all right with Jerry, hopes —I think untruthfully—that we may meet again, and goes.

Jerry—looks about my own age, wears rather defiant aspect and spectacles with preternaturally convex lenses—favours direct method of approach and says instantly that he understands that I write.

Yes, I do.

Then the one thing that those whom he designates as "All You People" have got to realise is that we must all go on *exactly as usual*. If we are novelists, we must go on writing novels; if poets, write poetry just as before; if our line happens to be light journalism, then let it still be light journalism. But keep away from war topics. Not a word about war.

And what about lecturing, I enquire?

Lecture by all means, replies Jerry benevolently.

Read up something about the past—not history, better keep away from history—but what about such things as Conchology, Philately, the position of Woman in the Ice Age, and so on. Anything, in fact, which may suggest itself to us that has no bearing whatever on the present international situation.

I feel obliged to point out to Jerry that the present international situation is what most people, at the moment, wish to know about.

Jerry taps on his writing-desk very imperatively indeed and tells me that All You People are the same. All anxious to do something about the war. Well, we mustn't. We must keep right out of it. Forget about it. Go on writing just as though it didn't exist.

Cannot, at this, do less than point out to Jerry that most of us are writing with a view to earning our living and those of our dependents, and this is difficult enough already without deliberately avoiding the only topic which is likely, at the present juncture, to lead to selling our works.

It won't do, says Jerry, shaking his head, it won't do at all. Authors, poets, artists—(can

[265]

see that the word he really has in mind is riff-raff)—and All You People must really come into line and be content to carry on exactly as usual. Otherwise, simply doing more harm than good.

Am by this time more than convinced that Jerry has no work of national significance to offer me, and that I had better take my leave. Final flicker of spirit leads me to ask whether he realises that it is very difficult indeed to find a market for any writings just now, and Jerry replies off-handedly that, of course, the paper shortage *is* very severe and will get much worse —much, much worse.

At the same time it is quite on the cards that people will take to reading when they find there's absolutely nothing else to do. Old ladies, for instance, or women who are too idle and incompetent to do any war work. They may quite likely take to reading light novels in the long evenings, so as to help kill time. So long as I remember to carry on just exactly as I should if we weren't at war at all, Jerry feels sure that I shall be quite all right.

Can only get up and say Goodbye without informing him that I differ from this conclusion

*All you people must really come into line and carry
on exactly as usual.*

root and branch, and Jerry shakes hands with me with the utmost heartiness, driving ring inherited from great-aunt Julia into my finger with extremely painful violence.

Goodbye, he says, he is only too glad to have been of any help to me, and if I want advice on any other point I am not to hesitate for one moment to come and see him again.

Walk out completely dazed, with result that I pay no heed to my direction and find myself almost at once on ground floor, opposite entrance, without the slightest idea of how I got there.

(*Note:* Promptings of the unconscious, when it comes to questions of direction, incomparably superior to those of the conscious mind. Have serious thoughts of working this up into interesting article for any publication specialising in Psychology Made Easy.)

Rain pours down; I have no umbrella and am reluctantly compelled to seek shelter in a tea-shop where I ask for coffee and get some with skin on it. Tell myself in a fury that this could never happen in America, or any other country except England.

In spite of this, am deeply dejected at the

thought that the chances of my serving my country are apparently non-existent.

November 2nd.—Tremendous outbreak of knitting overtakes the underworld—cannot say why or how. Society Deb. works exclusively in Air-Force blue, and Muriel—who alone can understand her muttered utterances—reports that Jennifer has never done any knitting before and isn't really any good at it, but her maid undoes it all when she has a night at home and knits it up again before Jennifer wakes.

Muriel is herself at work on a Balaclava helmet, elderly Messenger very busy with navy-blue which it is thought will turn into socks sooner or later, and everybody compares stitches, needles and patterns. Mrs. Peacock (reappeared, leg now well again but she still has tendency to retire to upturned box as often as possible) knits very rapidly and continuously but says nothing, until she privately reveals to me that she is merely engaged on shawl for prospective grandchild but does not like to talk about it as it seems unpatriotic.

Am sympathetic about grandchild, but inwardly rather overcome as Mrs. P. is obviously contemporary of my own and have not hitherto viewed myself as potential grandmother, but quite see that better accustom myself to this idea as soon as possible.

(Have not yet succeeded in doing so, all the same.)

Serena, also knitting—stout khaki muffler, which she says is all she can manage, and even so, broader at one end than at the other—comes and leans against Canteen counter at slack moments and tells me that she doesn't know what to do about J. L. If his novel had been accepted by publishers, she declares, it would all be quite easy because she wouldn't mind hurting his feelings, but with publishers proving discouraging and poor J. L. in deepest depression, it is, says Serena, practically impossible to say No.

Is she, then, engaged to him?

Oh *no*, says Serena, looking horrified.

But is she going to marry him?

Serena doesn't know. Probably *not*.

Remind myself that standards have changed and that I must be modern-minded, and enquire boldly whether Serena is considering having An Affair with J. L.

[269]

Serena looks unspeakably shocked and assures me that she isn't like that *at all*. She is very old-fashioned, and so are all her friends, and nowadays it's a wedding ring or nothing.

Am completely taken aback and realise that I have, once again, entirely failed to keep abreast of the times.

Apologise to Serena, who replies that of course it's all right and she knows that in post-last-war and pre-this-war days, people had some rather odd ideas, but they all went out with the nineteen-twenties.

Can see that, if not literally a grandmother, am definitely so in spiritual sense.

Serena then presents further, and totally unrelated, problem for my consideration. It appears that Commandant of Stretcher-party has recently resigned position in order to take up service abroad and those to whom he has given series of excellent and practical lectures have made him presentation of fountain-pen and pencil in red morocco case.

Farewell speeches have been exchanged, and red morocco case appreciatively acknowledged.

Now, however, Stretcher-party Commandant

has suddenly reappeared, having been medically rejected for service abroad, and Serena feels that morocco case is probably a source of embarrassment to him.

Can make no constructive comments about this whatever, and simply tell her that next move—if any—rests entirely with Commandant of Stretcher-party.

Interruption occurs in the person of old Mrs. Winter-Gammon who comes up and asks me what I can suggest for an old lady's supper.

Steak-pudding, sausages-and-mashed or spaghetti? Mrs. W.-G. shakes her curls and screws up her eyes and says gaily, No, no, no—it's very naughty of her to say so, but none of it sounds attractive. She will have a teeny drop of soup and some brown bread-and-butter.

Collect this slender meal and place it before her, and she says that will last her until breakfast-time next morning. Her dear Edgar used to get quite worried sometimes, and tell her that she didn't eat more than a sparrow, but to this she had only one answer: Dearest one, you forget how tiny I am. I don't need more than a sparrow would. All I ask is that what I *do* have

[271]

shall be daintily cooked and served. A vase of
flowers on the table, a fringed doiley or two,
and I'm every bit as happy with a crust of bread
and an apple as I could be with a banquet. In
fact, happier.

Cannot think of any reply whatever to all
this and merely look blankly at Granny Bo-
Peep, who smiles roguishly and informs me that
she believes I'm only half-awake. (Feel that
she might just as well have said half-witted.)

Can quite understand why Serena, who has
also listened to Mrs. W.-G., now abruptly declares that she wants cold beef, pickles and
toasted cheese for *her* supper.

Mrs. W.-G.—still immovable at counter—
asks how I found Devonshire, and what poor
Blanche is doing, and whether my husband
doesn't miss me dreadfully. She herself, so long
as beloved Edgar was with her, was always beside him. He often said that she knew more
about his work than he did himself. That, of
course, was nonsense—her talents, if she had
any at all, were just the little humble domestic
ones. She made their home as cosy as she could
—a touch here, another one there—a few little

[272]

artistic contrivances—and above all, a smile. Whatever happened, she was determined that Edgar should always see a smiling face. With that end in view, Mrs. W.-G. used to have a small mirror hanging up over her desk so that every time she raised her eyes she could see herself and make sure that the smile was *there*. If it wasn't, she just said to herself, Now, Pussy, what are you about? and went on looking, until the smile *was* there.

Am suddenly inspired to enquire of old Mrs. W.-G. what first occasioned her to share a flat with Aunt Blanche. Can never remember receiving any explanation on the point from Aunt Blanche herself, and am totally at a loss to understand why anyone should ever have wished to pursue joint existence with Granny Bo-Peep and her smile.

Ah, says Mrs. W.-G., a dear mutual friend —now Passed On—came to her, some years ago, and suggested the whole idea. Poor Blanche, in the opinion of the mutual friend, needed Taking Out of Herself. *Why* the friend thought that Mrs. W.-G. was the right person to accomplish this, she cannot pretend to guess

—but so it was. And somehow or other—and it's no use my asking Mrs. W.-G. to explain, because she just doesn't know how it's done herself—but *somehow* or other, dear old Blanche did seem to grow brighter and to realise something of the sheer *fun* of thinking about other people, instead of about one's own little troubles. She must just have caught it, like the measles, cries Granny Bo-Peep merrily. People have always told her that she has such an infectious chuckle, and she simply can't help seeing the funny side of things. So she can only suppose that Blanche—bless her—somehow took the infection.

Then came the war, and Mrs. W.-G. instantly decided that she was nothing but a worthless old woman and must go and offer her services, and the Commandant to whom she offered them—not this one, but quite another one, now doing something entirely different in another part of England altogether—simply replied: Pussy, I only wish I was as plucky, as efficient, as cheery, and as magnificent as you are. Will you drive an ambulance?

I will, replied Mrs. W.-G., drive anything, anywhere and at any time whatsoever.

[274]

Feel that any comment I could make on this would only be in the nature of an anti-climax and am immensely relieved when Scottish voice in my ear asks would I not take over the tea-pot for a wee while?

I would, and I do.

Mysterious behaviour of tea, which is alternately black as ink and strong as death, or revoltingly pallid and with tea-leaves floating about unsymmetrically on the surface of the cup. Can see that more intelligent management of hot-water supply would remedy both states of affairs, but all experiments produce unsatisfactory results and am again compelled to recognise my own inefficiency, so unlike general competence of Granny Bo-Peep.

Dispense tea briskly for nearly an hour, discuss menu with cashier—rather good-looking Jewess—who agrees with me that it lacks variety.

Why not, I ask, have kippers, always popular? Or fish-cakes. Jewess agrees to kippers but says a fish-cake isn't a thing to eat out.

Spend some minutes in wondering what she means, until it is borne in on me that she, probably rightly, feels it desirable to have some per-

[275]

sonal knowledge as to the ingredients of fish-cakes before embarking on them.

Cannot think why imagination passes from fish-cakes to Belgrave Square ballroom somewhere about the year 1912, and myself in the company of young Guardsman—lost sight of for many years, and in any case, no longer either young or in the Guards. Realise very slowly that gramophone record of "Merry Widow" waltz is now roaring through the Canteen, and accounts for all.

Am struck by paradoxical thought that youth is by no means the happiest time of life, but that most of the rest of life is tinged by regret for its passing, and wonder what old age will feel like, in this respect. (Shall no doubt discover very shortly.)

Girl with lovely red hair—name unknown—comes up for customary meal of hot milk and one digestive biscuit and tells me that I look very profound.

I say Yes, I *am* very profound, and was thinking about Time.

Am rather astonished and greatly impressed when she calmly returns that she often thinks

[276]

Jewess agrees to kippers, but says a fish-cake isn't a thing to eat out.

about Time herself, and has read through the whole of J. W. Dunne's book.

Did she understand it?

Well, the first two and a half pages she understood perfectly. The whole thing seemed to her so simple that she was unable to suppose that even a baby wouldn't understand it.

Then, all of a sudden, she found she wasn't understanding it any more. Complete impossibility of knowing at what page, paragraph, or even sentence, this inability first overtook her. It just was *like* that. At one minute she was understanding it all perfectly—at the next, all was incomprehensible.

Can only inform her that my own experiences with J. W. D. have been identical, except that I think I only understood the first two, *not* two and a half pages.

Decide—as often before—that one of these days I shall tackle Time and J. W. D. all over again.

In the meanwhile, fresh vogue for tea has overtaken denizens of the underworld, and I deal with it accordingly.

Nine O'clock News comes and goes unheard

[277]

by me, and probably by most other people owing to surrounding din. Serena drifts up later and informs us that Lord Nuffield has been appointed Director-General of Maintenance in Air Ministry. Have idle thoughts of asking him whether he would like capable, willing and efficient secretary, and am just receiving urgent pre-paid telegram from him begging me to accept the post at once when I discover that the milk has given out and supply ought to have been renewed from the kitchen ten minutes ago.

Go back to flat soon afterwards, write letter to Robert and tell him that nothing has as yet materialised from Ministry of Information—which I prefer to saying that repeated applications have proved quite unavailing—but that I am still serving at Canteen, and that everybody seems fairly hopeful.

Reflect, whilst going to bed, that I am thoroughly tired of all my clothes and cannot afford new ones.

November 4th.—Am rung up, rather to my astonishment, by Literary Agent, wishing to know What I Am Doing.

[278]

Well, I am in touch with the Ministry of Information, and also doing voluntary work at a Canteen every night. At the same time, if he wishes to suggest that I should use my pen for the benefit of the country . . .

No, he hasn't anything of that kind to suggest. On the contrary. The best thing I can do is just carry on exactly as usual, and no doubt I am at work on a new novel at this very moment.

I urge that it's very difficult to give one's mind to a new novel under present conditions, and Literary Agent agrees that doubtless this is so, but it is my plain duty to make the attempt. He has said the same thing to *all* his authors.

Reflection occurs to me later, though not, unfortunately, at moment of conversation, that if all of them take his advice the literary market will be completely swamped with novels in quite a short time, and authors' chances of making a living, already very precarious, will cease to exist at all.

Spend some time at writing-desk, under hazy impression that I am thinking out a new novel.

Discover at the end of two hours that I have achieved rather spirited little drawing on cover of telephone book of man in a fez—slightly less good representation of rustic cottage, Tudor style, front elevation, on envelope of Aunt Blanche's last letter—also written two cheques meeting long-overdue accounts—smoked (apparently) several cigarettes, of which I have no recollection whatever, and carefully cut out newspaper advertisement of Fleecy-lined Coats with Becoming Hoods—which I have no intention whatever of purchasing.

New novel remains wholly elusive.

Telephone rings again: on raising receiver become aware of tremendous pandemonium of sound which tells me instantly that this must be the Adelphi underworld.

It is.

May Serena bring round J. L. for a drink at about 6.30 this evening? He would like to talk about his new novel. Reply mirthlessly that perhaps he would also like to hear about mine—but this cynical reference wasted, as Serena only replies What? and adds Blast this place, it's like a rookery, only worse.

Tell her that it doesn't matter, and I can tell her later, and she suggests that if I scream straight into the mouthpiece very loud, she'll probably be able to hear—but I again assure her that this would be wasted energy.

We end conversation—if conversation it can be called—with reciprocal assurances that we shall look forward to meeting at my flat, 6.30 P.M., with J. L. in Serena's train.

Go to wine merchant at corner of the street and tell him that I require an Amontillado—which is the only name I know in the sherry world—and that I hope he has some in stock.

Well—Amontillado is now very, very difficult to obtain—(knew perfectly well he was going to say this)—but he *thinks* he can supply me. That is, if I do not require it in any very great quantity.

Had actually only considered purchasing a single bottle but have not now got the face to say so, and reply that two bottles will satisfy me *for the moment*. (Distinct implication here that I shall be back in about an hour's time for several more.)

Ah, then in *that* case—says wine merchant

[281]

with quite unabated suavity of manner, for which I think highly of him.

We hold very brief discussion as to the degree of dryness required in sherry, in which I hope I produce an effect of knowing the subject *à fond*—and I pay for my two bottles and am told that they will be delivered within a few moments at my door—which in fact they are.

Proceed to purchase of small cheese biscuits, and hope that Serena will think I have done her credit.

Canteen duty follows—very uneventful interlude. Serena not on duty, and Granny Bo-Peep visible only in the distance where she is—apparently—relating the story of her life to group of Decontamination men who seem, unaccountably, to find it interesting.

Mrs. Peacock tells me that Old Moore predicted the war and said that it would come to an end in 1940. Did he, whilst about it, say in what month? Mrs. Peacock thinks he said November, but is not sure, and I suggest that he was mixing it up with the Great War, at which she seems hurt.

[282]

Shift comes to an end at six o'clock, and I leave underworld thinking how best to arrange seating for three people in flat sitting-room, which is scarcely large enough to contain two with any comfort, when folding-table is extended to receive Amontillado and glasses.

Find flat door wide open, curtains drawn—(no brown paper)—lamp and fire burning merrily, and Serena entertaining J. L., Muriel and unknown young man of film-star appearance. Table has been set up, Amontillado opened, and agreeable haze of cigarette-smoke fills the air.

Serena says It's lovely that I've come at last, and she hopes it's all right, she thought I should wish them to have a drink, and couldn't she pour one out for me?

Agree that she could, and congratulate myself inwardly on having dealt with lip-stick, powder and pocket comb on the stairs.

Ensuing party proves gay and amusing, and I enter into conversation with film-star young man, who tells me that he has been reading J. L.'s novel in typescript and thinks it very good. Have I seen it?

[283]

No, I've only heard about it from Serena. What is it called?

It is called *Poached Eggs to the Marble Arch*.

At this I bend my head appreciatively, as if to say that's exactly the sort of name I should have *expected* from a really good modern novelist, and then have the wind taken out of my sails when young film-star observes thoughtfully that he thinks it's an utterly vague and off-putting title. But, he adds candidly, he isn't absolutely sure he's got it right. It might be *Poached Eggs* ON *the Marble Arch*, or even *Poached Eggs* AT *the Marble Arch*.

Conversation then becomes general, and Serena and Muriel talk about their war service and I say nothing about mine—not from modesty but because Canteen work very unimpressive—and film-star young man reveals that he has just joined the Air Force Reserve, and isn't a film-star at all but a psychiatrist, and that ever since war started he has had no patients at all as most of the ones he had before were children who have been sent away from London.

Enquire at once whether he knows Rose, in very similar position to his own, and he says he knows her well by name. This does not, really, get us very much further.

J. L. looks, as before, intelligent and melancholy and latter expression seems to be merely deepened by Amontillado. Curiously opposite effect is produced on myself and I become unusually articulate and—I think—very witty about the Ministry of Information.

This conviction deepened every moment by shrieks of laughter from Serena and Muriel, definite appearance of amusement on face which still seems to me that of a film-star, and even faint smiles from J. L.

Am regretful when S. and M. declare that duty now calls them to the Adelphi. (It must, to be accurate, have been calling for rather more than an hour, as both were due there at seven o'clock.)

They take some time to make their farewells, and are escorted away by pseudo film-star, who thanks me very earnestly for having invited him. Do not, naturally, point out to him that I didn't do so, and have, in fact, no idea who did.

J. L. to my astonishment enquires whether

I am, by any possible chance, free for dinner this evening?

Am entirely free, and say so instantly, and J. L. invites me to come and dine somewhere with him at once and go on afterwards to Arts Club of which he is a member, and listen to Ridgeway's Late Joys. They sing Victorian songs and the audience joins in the choruses.

Am entranced at this prospect and only hope that effect of Amontillado will not have worn off by the time we get there, as should certainly join in choruses, Victorian or otherwise, far better if still under its influence.

J. L. and I depart forthwith into the black-out, and are compelled to cling to one another as we go, and even so do not escape minor collisions with sandbags and kindly expressed, but firm, rebuke from the police for displaying electric-torch beams too freely.

J. L. takes me to nice little restaurant and orders excellent dinner, and then talks to me about Serena.

He is, he admits, practically in despair about Serena. She has charm, she has intelligence, she has brains, she has looks—but would marriage with her be a hundred per cent success?

Can only tell him that I really have no idea, and that very few marriages *are* a hundred per cent success, but that on the other hand most people would think even seventy-five per cent quite handsome. Is he, if I may ask, engaged to Serena?

Oh dear no.

Has he—if he doesn't mind my asking—asked Serena to be engaged to him.

Well, yes and no.

Can only look at him in despair, and reflect with no originality whatever that Things have Changed in the last twenty years.

J. L. continues to maunder, but breaks off to ask what I would like to drink, and to hold quite animated discussion about Alsatian wine with the wine-waiter—then relapses into distress and refers to Serena as being at once the Worst and the Best Thing in his life.

Can see that nothing I say will make the slightest impression on him and that I may just as well save myself exertion of thinking by merely looking interested and sympathetic.

This succeeds well until J. L. suddenly bends forward and enquires earnestly whether I don't feel that Serena is too highly-strung to be the ideal wife for a writer. I inform him in return, without hesitation, that the point seems to me quite insignificant and that what really disturbs me is the conviction that writers are too egotistical to make ideal husbands for anybody.

J. L. instantly agrees with me but is evidently quite fatalistic about it and has no intention whatever of reforming.

Can only suggest to him that perhaps we had better start for Late Joys or we shall be late.

He agrees amiably and cheers up more and more as evening progresses—just as well, as I am perfectly enraptured by beautifully-produced performance of the Joys and too much absorbed to pay any attention to him even if suicidal tendencies should develop.

Instead, however, J. L. joins in chorus to "See Me Dance the Polka" and "Her Golden Hair Was Hanging Down Her Back" in unexpectedly powerful baritone, and we drink beer and become gayer and gayer until reluctantly compelled to leave theatre.

November 9th.—Bomb Explosion in Munich Beer-Hall reported, apparently timed to coincide with speech by Hitler and to destroy him

J. L. suddenly bends forward and enquires earnestly whether I don't feel that Serena is too highly-strung to be the ideal wife for a writer.

and numerous Nazi leaders seated immediately beneath spot where bomb was placed. Hitler said to have finished speech twenty minutes earlier than usual, and left Hall just—(from his point of view)—in time.

Hear all this from wireless at 8 A.M. and rush out into the Strand where posters tell me that Hess was amongst those killed, and I buy three newspapers and see that Hess is only *reported* killed. Can only say that instincts of Christianity and civilisation alike are severely tried, and am by no means prepared to state that they emerge victorious.

Have invited Lady Blowfield to lunch at Club as small return for past hospitality and also with faint hope of her eventually inducing Sir Archibald to suggest war job for me, and proceed there by bus, which fails to materialise for at least twenty minutes and is then boarded by about five hundred more people than it can possibly accommodate.

Situation very reminiscent of 1914 and succeeding years.

Hess resurrected on posters.

Reach Club just before one, am told by hall

porter that my guest has not yet arrived and go
to upstairs drawing-room, which is filled with
very, very old ladies in purple wool cardigans,
and exceedingly young ones in slacks. No
golden mean achieved between youth and age,
excepting myself.

Small room off drawing-room contains wireless, to which I hasten, and find fearfully dis-
traught-looking member—grey hair all over the
place and spectacles on the floor—who glances
at me and tells me imperatively to Hush!

I do Hush, to the extent of not daring even
to sit down on a chair, and One O'clock News
repeats the information that Hitler left Munich
Beer-Hall exactly fifteen minutes before bomb
exploded.

At this, grey-haired member astounds me by
wringing her hands—have never seen this done
before in real earnest—and emits a sort of
frantic wail to the effect that it's dreadful—
dreadful! That he should just have missed it
by quarter of an hour! Why, oh, why couldn't
they have timed it better?

Moral conflict assails me once more at this,
since I am undeniably in sympathy with her, but

Grey-haired member astounds me by wringing her hands.

at the same time rather shattered by her unusual outspokenness. No comment fortunately necessary, or even possible, as she desperately increases volume of wireless to bellowing-point, then extinguishes it with equal lack of moderation.

Can see that she is in totally irresponsible frame of mind and feel very sorry for her.

Try to convey this by a look when News is over, and am only too successful as she at once pours out a torrent of rather disconnected phrases, and ends up by asking what my views are.

There will, I assure her, be a revolution in Germany very soon.

She receives this not-very-novel theory with staring eyes and enquires further whether It will come from the top, or from the bottom.

Both, I reply without hesitation, and leave the room before she has time to say more.

Lady Blowfield awaits me—hat with a black feather, very *good*-looking fur cape, and customary air of permanent anxiety—and we exchange greetings and references—moderate at least in tone—to Munich explosion, Hess being authoritatively declared alive and unhurt on the strength of responsible newspapers seen by Lady Blowfield.

Offer her sherry which she declines—am rather sorry, as I should have liked some myself but feel it now quite out of the question— and we proceed to dining-room.

Has she, I ask, any news about the war other than that which is officially handed out to all of us?

Lady Blowfield at once replies that Gitnik, whom I shall remember meeting, has flown to Paris and that therefore she has not seen him. He is, I shall naturally understand, her chief authority on world affairs—but failing him, Archibald has a certain amount of inside information—in a comparatively small way— and he has said that, in his opinion, the war will begin very soon now.

Am much dejected by this implication, although I—like everybody else—have frequently said myself that It isn't yet Started.

Has Sir Archibald given any intimation of the place or time selected for the opening of hostilities?

Lady Blowfield shakes her head and says that Holland is in great danger, so is Belgium, so are Finland and Sweden. At the same time it is perfectly certain that Hitler's *real* objective is England, and he is likely to launch a tremendous air-attack against not only London, but the whole of the country. It is nonsense—wishful thinking, in fact—to suggest that winter will make any difference. Weather will have nothing to do with it. Modern aircraft can afford to ignore *all* weather conditions.

Has Lady Blowfield any information at all as to when this attack may be expected?

Lady Blowfield—not unreasonably—says that it won't be *expected* at all.

Conversation, to my relief, is here interrupted by prosaic enquiry from waitress as to our requirements and I urge grape-fruit and braised chicken on Lady Blowfield and again suggest drink. Would willingly stand her entire bottle of anything at all, in the hope of cheering her up. She rejects all intoxicants, however, and sips cold water.

What, she wishes to know, am I doing with my time? Am I writing anything? Archibald, no later than the day before yesterday, wished to know whether I was writing anything in particular, and whether I realised how useful I could be in placing before the public points which it was desirable for them to know.

Feel more hopeful at this, and ask what points?

There is, replies Lady Blowfield, the question of Root Vegetables. English housewives do not make the best use of these, in cooking. An attractive pamphlet on the subject of Root Vegetables might do a lot just now.

Can only suppose that I look as unenthusiastic as I feel, since she adds, with rather disappointed expression, that if I don't care about *that*, there is a real need, at the moment, for literature that shall be informative, helpful and at the same time amusing, about National Economy. How to avoid waste in the small household, for instance.

Tell her that if I knew how to avoid waste in the small household, I should find myself in a very different position financially from that in which I am at present, and Lady Blowfield then shifts her ground completely and suggests that I should Read It Up.

She will send me one or two little booklets, if I like. I have the honesty to admit in reply that I have, in the past, obtained numbers of little booklets, mostly at Women's Institutes, and have even read some of them, but cannot feel that the contents have ever altered the course of my days.

Ah, says Lady Blowfield darkly, perhaps not *now*, but when the war is over—though heaven alone knows when that may be—*then* I shall realise how difficult mere *existence* is going to be, and that all life will have to be reorganised into something very, very different from anything we have ever known before. Have frequently thought and said the same thing myself, but am nevertheless depressed when I hear it from Lady Blowfield. (This quite unreasonable, especially as I hold definite opinion that entire readjustment of present social system is desirable from every point of view.)

Shall we, I next suggest with an air of originality, try and forget about the war and talk about something entirely different? Lady Blowfield, though seeming astonished, agrees and at once asks me if by any chance I know of

[295]

a really good kitchen-maid—she believes they are easier to find now—as hers is leaving to be married.

(If this is part of Lady Blowfield's idea of preparing for entirely reorganised scheme of life, can only say that it fails to coincide with mine.)

Am compelled to admit that I am a broken reed indeed as regards kitchen-maids, and enquire whether Lady Blowfield has seen *George and Margaret*.

No, she says, who are George and Margaret? Do I mean Daisy Herrick-Delaney and poor dear Lord George?

Explain what I do mean.

She has *not* seen *George and Margaret* and does not sound, even after I have assured her that it is very amusing, as if she either wished or intended to do so.

Fortunately recollect at this stage that the Blowfields are friends of Robert's married sister in Kanya—whom I have only met twice and scarcely know—and we discuss her and her children—whom I have never met at all—for the remainder of luncheon.

Coffee subsequently served in library is excellent and Lady Blowfield compliments me on it, and says how rare it is to find good coffee, and I agree whole-heartedly and feel that some sort of *rapprochement* may yet take place between us.

If so, however, it must be deferred to another occasion, as Lady Blowfield looks at her watch, screams faintly, and asserts that her Committee will be expecting her at this very moment and she must Fly.

She does fly—though not rapidly—and I retire to Silence Room with every intention of writing out brief, but at the same time complete, synopsis of new novel.

Two members are already seated in Silence Room, hissing quietly at one another, but lapse into frustrated silence at my entrance.

Sit down at writing-table with my back to them but can feel waves of resentment still emanating towards me.

Tell myself quite firmly that this is Great Nonsense, and that anyway they can perfectly well go and talk somewhere which *isn't* a Silence Room, and that I really must give my mind to proposed synopsis.

Do so, for what seems like three weeks.

Customary pen-and-ink drawings result and lead me to wonder, without much conviction, whether I have perhaps mistaken my vocation and should have done better as black-and-white artist. Brief dream ensues of myself in trousers, smock and large black bow, figuring in Bohemian life on the *rive gauche* at the age of twenty-two. Have just been escorted by group of enthusiastic fellow students to see several of my own works of art exhibited at the Salon, when recollections of Robert and the children—cannot say why or how—suddenly come before me, and I realise that all are quite unsuitable figures in scene that Fancy has depicted.

Revert once more to synopsis.

Cannot imagine why concentration should prove next door to impossible, until instinct tells me that psychic atmosphere is again distinctly hostile, and that the hissing members are probably wishing I would drop down dead.

Look cautiously round for them, and see that one is sleeping heavily and the other has completely disappeared.

(How? Have not heard door either open or shut. Have evidently concentrated better

[298]

than I supposed. But *on what*? Answer comes
there none.)

Inspiration, without a word of warning,
descends upon me and I evolve short and
rather flippant topical article which may reasonably be expected to bring me in a small
sum of money, fortunately payable in guineas,
not pounds.

Am highly elated—frame of mind which
will undoubtedly undergo total eclipse on re-
reading article in type—and return to Buckingham Street. Remember quite a long while
afterwards that projected synopsis is still non-
existent.

Find flat occupied, on my arrival, by Serena
—face a curious shade of green—who says that
she feels rather like death and has leave of absence for an hour in order to get into the fresh
air. This she has evidently elected to do by putting on electric fire, shutting the window, boil-
ing the kettle and drinking quantities of very
strong tea.

Commiserate with her, and suggest that conditions under which she is serving the country
are both very strenuous and extremely unhy-

gienic and that she may shortly be expected to break down under them.

Serena says Yes, she quite agrees.

Then what about trying something else?

Yes, replies Serena, but *what*? Everybody she knows, practically, is trying to Get Into Something, and everybody is being told that, whilst everybody is urgently needed, nobody can be given any work at the moment. Quite highly qualified persons are, she asserts, begging and imploring to be allowed to scrub floors and wash dishes without pay, but nobody will have them.

Am obliged to admit that this is only too true.

And there is another thing, says Serena. The moment—the very moment—that she leaves her A.R.P.,[1] there will be an air-raid over London. Then she will have had all these weeks and weeks of waiting about for nothing, and will just have to cower in a basement like everybody else while old Granny Bo-Peep is getting all the bombs.

Assure Serena that, while I know what she

[1] Air Raid Precautions.

means—which I do—it seems to me an absolute certainty that Granny Bo-Peep will succeed in getting well into the middle of whatever calamity may occur, and in getting out of it again with unimpaired spirits and increased prestige.

I therefore suggest that Serena may put her out of her calculations altogether.

Serena—surely rather exasperatingly?—declares that she wasn't really thinking what she was saying, and Granny Bo-Peep doesn't come into it at all.

Then what does?

Serena's only reply is to weep.

Am very sorry for her, tell her so, give her a kiss, suggest brandy, all to no avail. Remember Spartan theory many times met with both in literature and in life, that hysterical tendencies can be instantly checked by short, sharp word of command or, in extreme cases, severe slap. Do not feel inclined for second alternative, but apply the first—with the sole result that Serena cries much harder than before.

Spartan theory definitely discredited.

Electric bell is heard from below, and Serena

says Oh, good heavens, is someone coming! and rushes into the bedroom.

Someone turns out to be The Times Book Club, usually content to leave books in hall but opportunely inspired on this occasion to come up the stairs and demand threepence.

This I bestow on him and we exchange brief phrases about the weather—wet—the war—not yet really begun—and Hitler's recent escape from assassination—better luck next time. (This last contribution from Times Book Club, but endorsed by myself.)

Times Book Club clatters away again, and I look at what he has brought—murder story by Nicholas Blake, which I am delighted to see, and historical novel by author unknown but well spoken of in reviews.

Serena emerges again—nose powdered until analogy with Monte Rosa in a snowstorm is irresistibly suggested, but naturally keep it to myself—and says she is very sorry indeed, she's quite all right now and she can't imagine what made her so idiotic.

Could it, I hint, by any possible chance be over-fatigue and lack of adequate sleep and fresh air?

Serena says that has nothing to do with it, and I think it inadvisable to dispute the point.

She again consults me about J. L. (who has so recently consulted me about her) and I again find it wiser to remain silent while she explains how difficult it all is and admits to conviction that whatever they decide, both are certain to be wretched.

She then becomes much more cheerful, tells me how kind and helpful I have been, and takes affectionate farewell.

Indulge in philosophical reflections on general feminine inability to endure prolonged strain without emotional collapse.

November 11th.—Armistice Day, giving rise to a good many thoughts regarding both past and present. Future, to my mind, better left to itself, but this view evidently not universally held, as letters pour out from daily and weekly Press full of suggestions as to eventual peace terms and reorganisation of the world in general.

Telephone to Robert, who says nothing in particular but seems pleased to hear my voice.

Interesting, but rather academic, letter from Robin full of references to New Ideology but omitting any reply to really very urgent enquiry from myself regarding new winter vests.

November 12th.—Take afternoon duty instead of evening at Canteen and learn that Society Deb. has developed signs of approaching nervous breakdown and been taken away by her mother. Girl with curls—Muriel—has disappeared, unnoticed by anybody at all, until she is required to take a car to Liverpool Street station, when hue and cry begins and Serena finally admits that Muriel has a fearful cold and went home to bed three days ago without notifying anybody at all.

Defence offered by Serena is to the effect that Muriel thought, as she wasn't doing anything, she could easily go and come back again unperceived.

Various members of personnel are likewise wilting, and Serena looks greener than ever.

Commandant can be heard raging at Darling behind closed door of office, and is said to have uttered to the effect that if there's any more of this rank insubordination she is going to hand in her resignation. In fact she would do so at once, if she didn't happen to realise, as nobody else appears to do, that England Is At War.

Have serious thoughts of asking her whether she hasn't heard anybody say that It Hasn't yet Started? If not, this establishes a record.

Afternoon very slack and principal activities consist in recommending the bread-and-butter and toast, which can honestly be done, to all enquirers—saying as little as possible about the buns—and discouraging all approaches to jam tarts.

Mrs. Peacock offers me half-seat on her box, which I accept, and we look at new copy of very modern illustrated weekly, full of excellent photographs. Also read with passionate interest Correspondence Column almost entirely devoted to discussion of recent issue which apparently featured pictures considered by two-thirds of its readers to be highly improper, and by the remainder, artistic in the extreme.

Mrs. P. and I are at one in our regret that neither of us saw this deplorable contribution, and go so far as to wonder if it is too late to get hold of a copy.

[305]

Not, says Mrs. P., that she *likes* that kind of thing—very far from it—but one can't help wondering how far the Press will go nowadays, and she hadn't realised that there was anything left which would shock anybody.

Am less pessimistic than she is about this, but acknowledge that, although not particularly interested on my own account, I feel that one might as well see what is being put before the younger generation.

Having delivered ourselves of these creditable sentiments, Mrs. P. and I look at one another, both begin to laugh, and admit candidly distressing fact that both of us are definitely curious.

Mrs. P. then recklessly advocates two cups of tea, which we forthwith obtain and prepare to drink whilst seated on up-ended sugar-box, but intense activity at counter instantly surges into being and requirements of hitherto non-existent clients rise rapidly to peak height.

By the time these have been dealt with, and used cups, plates and saucers collected and delivered to kitchen, cups of tea have grown cold and all desire for refreshment passed, and Mrs. P. says That's life all over, isn't it?

Return to Buckingham Street and find telephone message kindly taken down by caretaker, asking if I can lunch with Mr. Pearman to-morrow at one o'clock, and the house is No. 501 Sloane Street and can be found in the telephone book under name of Zonal.

Am utterly bewildered by entire transaction, having never, to my certain knowledge, heard either of Mr. Pearman or anyone called Zonal in my life, and Sloane Street address—Cadwallader House—conveying nothing whatever to me.

Enquire further details of caretaker.

She says apologetically that the line was very bad—she thinks the war has made a difference—and she asked for the name three times, but didn't like to go on.

Then she isn't quite certain that it *was* Pearman?

Well, no, she isn't. It *sounded* like that, the first time, but after that she didn't feel so sure, but she didn't like to go on bothering the lady.

[307]

Then was Mr. Pearman a lady? I enquire.

This perhaps not very intelligently worded but entirely comprehensible to caretaker, who replies at once that he was, and said that I should know who it was.

Adopt new line of enquiry and suggest that *Zonal* not very probable, in spite of being in telephone book.

But at this caretaker takes up definite stand. Zonal, Z for zebra, and she particularly asked to have it spelt because it seemed so funny but it's in the book all right—Brigadier A. B. Zonal—and Cadwallader House is that new block of flats up at the end.

Decide that the only thing to do is ring up Cadwallader House and ask for either Pearman or Zonal.

Line proves to be engaged.

I say that The Stars in their Courses are Fighting against Me, and caretaker, whom I have forgotten, looks extremely startled and suggests that perhaps I could ring up again later—which seems reasonable and obvious solution.

Make fresh attempt, am told that I am

speaking to the hall porter and enquire if there is anyone in the house of the name of Pearman—or, I add weakly, anything *like* that.

Will I spell the name?

I do.

No, the hall porter is very sorry, but he doesn't know of anybody of that name. I don't mean old Mrs. Wain, by any chance, do I?

Decline old Mrs. Wain, and suggest Zonal, of whom I am unable to give any other particulars than that he is a Brigadier.

Brigadier Zonal, says the porter, lives on the second floor, and his niece and her friend are staying there. The niece is Miss Armitage, and the other lady is Miss Fairmead.

Everything, I tell the porter, is explained. It *is* Miss Fairmead, of course, and would he ask her to speak to me? Porter—evidently man of imperturbable calm—replies Very good, madam, and I assure the caretaker—still hovering—that the name may have *sounded* like Mr. Pearman but was in reality Miss Fairmead. She replies that she *did* think of its being that at one time, but it didn't seem likely, somehow.

Consider this highly debatable point, but decide to let it drop and thank her instead for her trouble. (Trouble, actually, has been entirely mine.)

Explanation with Felicity Fairmead ensues. She is in London for two nights only, staying with Veronica Armitage, whom I don't know, in her turn staying with her uncle Brigadier Zonal, who has kindly offered hospitality to Felicity as well.

She and Veronica are leaving London the day after to-morrow, will I come and lunch to-morrow and meet Veronica? Also, naturally, the uncle—who will be my host.

Agree to all and say how glad I am to think of seeing Felicity, and should like to meet Veronica, of whom I have heard much. And, of course, the uncle.

November 13th.—Lunch—at Brigadier Zonal's expense—with Felicity, who is looking particularly nice in dark red with hair very well set. Veronica turns out pretty, with attractive manners, but is shrouded in blue woollen hood, attributable to violent neuralgia from which she is only just recovering.

Uncle not present after all, detained at War Office on urgent business.

Felicity asks respectfully after my war work—am obliged to disclaim anything of national significance—and immediately adds solicitous enquiry as to the state of my overdraft.

Can only reply that it is much what it always was—certainly no better—and my one idea is to economise in every possible way, and what about Felicity herself?

Nothing, declares Felicity, is paying any dividends at all. The last one she received was about twenty-five pounds less than it should have been and she paid it into the Bank and it was completely and immediately swallowed up by her overdraft. It just didn't exist any more. And the extraordinary thing is, she adds thoughtfully, that although this invariably happens whenever she pays anything into her Bank, the overdraft *never* gets any smaller. On the contrary.

She has asked her brother to explain this to her, and he has done so, but Felicity has failed to understand the explanation.

[311]

Perhaps, I suggest, the brother wasn't very clear?

Oh yes he was, absolutely. *He* knows a great deal about finance. It was just that Felicity hasn't got that kind of a mind.

Sympathise with her once more, admit—what she has known perfectly well ever since long-ago schooldays—that I haven't got that kind of mind either, and enquire what Veronica feels about it all.

Veronica thinks it's dreadful, and most depressing, and wouldn't it cheer us both up to go out shopping?

Personally, she has always found that shopping, even on a tiny scale, does one a great deal of good. She also feels that Trade ought to be encouraged.

Felicity and I readily agree to encourage Trade on a tiny scale. It is, I feel, imperative that I should get myself some stockings, and send Vicky a cake, and Felicity is prepared to encourage Trade to the extent of envelopes and a hair-net.

Veronica, in the absence of the uncle, presides over a most excellent lunch, concluding

with coffee, chocolates and cigarettes, and grati-
fies me by taking it for granted that we are on
Christian-name terms.

Felicity looks at me across the table and enquires with her eyebrows What I think of
Veronica? to which I reply, like Lord Burleigh,
with a nod.

We discuss air-raids—Germany does not
mean to attack London for fear of reprisals—
she *does* mean to attack London but not till the
spring—she hasn't yet decided whether to attack London or not. This war, in Felicity's
brother's opinion, is just as beastly as the last
one but will be shorter.

Enquire of Veronica what the uncle thinks,
and she answers that, being in the War Office,
he practically never tells one anything at all.
Whether from discretion, or because he doesn't
know, Veronica isn't sure—but inclines to the
latter theory.

Shortly afterwards Felicity puts on her hat
and extremely well-cut coat—which has the effect of making me feel that mine isn't cut at all
but just hangs on me—and we say goodbye to
Veronica and her blue hood.

[313]

Agreeable hour is spent in Harrods Stores, and I get Vicky's cake but substitute black felt hat and a check scarf for stockings. Felicity, who has recently had every opportunity of inspecting woollen hoods at close quarters, becomes passionately absorbed in specimens on counter and wishes to know if I think crochet or knitted would suit Veronica best. Do not hesitate to tell her that to me they look exactly alike and that, anyway, Veronica has a very nice one already.

Felicity agrees, but continues to inspect hoods none the less, and finally embarks on discussion with amiable shop-girl as to relative merits of knitting and crochet. She eventually admits that she is thinking of making a hood herself as friend with whom she is living as P.G. in the country does a great deal of knitting and Felicity does not like to be behindhand. Anyway, she adds, she isn't of any *use* to anybody, or doing anything to win the war.

Point out to her that very few of us *are* of any use, unless we can have babies or cook, and that none of us—so far as I can see—are doing anything to win the war. I also explain how different it will all be with Vicky's generation, and how competent they all are, able to cook and do house-work and make their own clothes. Felicity and I then find ourselves, cannot say how, sitting on green sofa in large paved black-and-white hall in the middle of Harrods, exchanging the most extraordinary reminiscences.

Felicity reminds me that she was never, in early youth, allowed to travel by herself, that she shared a lady's-maid with her sister, that she was never taught cooking, and never mended her own clothes.

Inform her in return that my mother's maid always used to do my hair for me, that I was considered industrious if I practised the piano for an hour in the morning, that nobody expected me to lift a finger on behalf of anybody else, except to write an occasional note of invitation, and that I had no idea how to make a bed or boil an egg until long after my twenty-first year.

We look at one another in the deepest dismay at these revelations of our past incompetence, and I say that it's no wonder the world is in the mess it's in to-day.

Felicity goes yet further, and tells me that, in a Revolution, our heads would be the first to go—and quite right too. But at this I jib and say that, although perhaps not really important assets to the community, we are, at least, able and willing to mend our ways and have in fact been learning to do so for years and years and years.

Felicity shakes her head and asserts that it's different for me, I've had two children and I write books. She herself is nothing but a cumberer of the ground and often contemplates her own utter uselessness without seeing any way of putting it right. She isn't intellectual, she isn't mechanically-minded, she isn't artistic, she isn't domesticated, she isn't particularly practical and she isn't even strong.

Can see, by Felicity's enormous eyes and distressed expression, that she would, in the event of the Revolution she predicts, betake herself to the scaffold almost as a matter of course.

Can only assure her, with the most absolute truth, that she possesses the inestimable advantages of being sympathetic, lovable and kind, and what the devil does she want more? Her

[316]

friends, I add very crossly, would hate to do without her, and are nothing if not grateful for the way in which she always cheers them up.

Felicity looks at me rather timidly—cannot imagine why—and suggests that I am tired and would it be too early for a cup of tea?

It wouldn't, and we go in search of one.

Realise quite suddenly, and for no reason whatever, that I have lost my gas-mask, in neat new leather case.

Had I, I agitatedly ask Felicity, got it on when I arrived at Cadwallader House?

Felicity is nearly certain I had. But she couldn't swear. In fact, she thinks she is really thinking of someone else. Can I remember if I had it on when I left home?

I am nearly certain I hadn't. But I couldn't swear either. Indeed, now I come to think of it, I am, after all, nearly certain I last saw it lying on my bed, with my National Registration Card.

Then is my National Registration Card lost too?

If it's on the bed in my flat, it isn't, and if it's not, then it is.

[317]

Agitated interval follows.

Felicity telephones to Cadwallader House—negative result—then to Buckingham Street caretaker, who goes up to look in bedroom but finds nothing, and I return to green sofa in black-and-white hall where places so recently occupied by Felicity and self are now taken up by three exquisite young creatures with lovely faces and no hats, smoking cigarettes and muttering to one another. They look at me witheringly when I enquire whether a gas-mask has been left there, and assure me that it hasn't, and as it is obviously inconceivable that they should be sitting on it unaware, can only apologise and retreat to enquire my way to Lost Property Office.

Am very kindly received, asked for all particulars and to give my name and address, and assured that I shall be notified if and when my gas-mask appears.

Felicity points out that loss of National Registration Card is much more serious and will necessitate a personal application to Caxton Hall, and even then I shall only get a temporary one issued. Can I remember when I saw mine last?

On my bed, with my gas-mask.

It couldn't have been, says Felicity, because caretaker says there's nothing there except a handkerchief and the laundry.

Then it must have got underneath the laundry.

Neither of us really believes this consoling theory, but it serves to buoy me up till I get home and find—exactly as I really expected—that nothing is underneath the laundry except the bed.

Extensive search follows and I find myself hunting madly in quite impossible spots, such as small enamelled box on mantelpiece, and biscuit tin which to my certain knowledge has never contained anything except biscuits.

Serena walks in whilst this is going on and expresses great dismay and commiseration, and offers to go at once to the underworld where she feels certain I must have left both gas-mask and National Registration Card.

Tell her that I never took either of them there in my life. It is well known that gas-mask is *not* obligatory within seven minutes' walk of home, and National Registration Card has lived in my bag.

[319]

Then have I, asks Serena with air of one inspired, *have* I looked in my bag?

Beg Serena, if she has nothing more helpful than this to suggest, to leave me to my search. *November 14th.*—Visit Caxton Hall, and am by no means sure that I ought not to do so in sackcloth with rope round my neck and ashes on my head.

Am not, however, the only delinquent. Elderly man stands beside me at counter where exhausted-looking official receives me, and tells a long story about having left card in pocket of his overcoat at his Club. He then turned his back for the space of five minutes and overcoat was instantly stolen.

Official begs him to fill in a form and warns him that he must pay a shilling for new Registration Card.

Elderly gentleman appalls me by replying that he cannot possibly do that. He hasn't got a shilling.

Official, unmoved, says he needn't pay it *yet*. It will do when he actually receives the new card. It will perhaps then, he adds kindly, be more convenient.

Elderly man appalls me by replying that he can't. That he hasn't got a shilling.

The only reply of elderly gentleman is to tell the story of his loss all over again—overcoat, card in pocket, Club, and theft during the five minutes in which his back was turned. Official listens with patience, although no enthusiasm, and I am assailed by ardent desire to enquire (*a*) name of Club, (*b*) how he can afford to pay his subscription to it if he hasn't got a shilling.

Endeavour to make my own story as brief as possible by way of contrast—can this be example of psychological phenomenon frequently referred to by dear Rose as compensating?—but find it difficult to make a good showing when I am obliged to admit that I have no idea either when or where National Registration Card was lost.

Nothing for it, says official, but to fill up a form and pay the sum of one shilling.

I do so; at the same time listen to quavering of very old person in bonnet and veil who succeeds me.

She relates, in very aggrieved tones, that she was paying a visit in Scotland when National Registration took place and her host and hostess

[321]

registered her without her knowledge or permission. This resulted in her being issued with a ration book. She does not wish for a ration book. She didn't ask for one, and won't have one.

Should like to hear much more of this, but official removes completed form, issues me with receipt for my shilling and informs me that I shall be communicated with in due course.

Can see no possible excuse for lingering and am obliged to leave Caxton Hall without learning what can be done for aged complainant. Reflect as I go upon extraordinary tolerance of British bureaucrats in general and recall everything I have heard or read as to their counterparts in Germany. This very nearly results in my being run over by bus in Victoria Street, and I am retrieved into safety by passer-by on the pavement, who reveals himself as Humphrey Holloway looking entirely unfamiliar in London clothes.

Look at him in idiotic astonishment, but eventually pull myself together and say that I'm delighted to meet him, and is he up here for long?

No, he doesn't think so. He has come up in order to find Something to Do as his services as Billeting Officer are now at an end.

Do not like to tell him how extremely slender I consider his chances of succeeding in this quest. Instead, I ask for news of Devonshire.

H. H. tells me that he saw Robert at church on Sunday and that he seemed all right.

Was Aunt Blanche there as well?

Yes, she was all right too.

And Marigold and Margery?

Both seemed to be quite all right.

Am rather discouraged by these laconic announcements and try to lure H. H. into details. Did Robert say anything about his A.R.P.[1] work?

He said that the woman who is helping him —H. H. can't remember her name—is a damned nuisance. Also that there's a village that hasn't got its gas-masks yet, but Robert thinks it will really have them before Christmas, with luck.

Not Mandeville Fitzwarren? I say, appalled.

H. H. thinks that was the name.

[1] Air Raid Precautions.

Can only reply that I hope the enemy won't find out about this before Christmas comes.

And what about Our Vicar and his wife and their evacuees?

They are, replies **H. H.**, settling down very nicely. At least the evacuees are. Our Vicar's Wife thought to be over-working, and looks very pale. She always seems, adds **H. H.**, to be here, there and everywhere. Parents of the evacuees all came down to see them the other day, and this necessitated fresh exertions from Our Vicar's Wife, but was said to have been successful on the whole.

Lady **B.** still has no patients to justify either Red Cross uniform or permanently-installed ambulance, and Miss Pankerton has organised a Keep Fit class in village every other evening, which is, says **H. H.** in tone of surprise, being well attended. He thinks that Aunt Blanche is one of the most regular members, together with Marigold and Margery. Do not inform him in return that Aunt Blanche has already told me by letter that Marigold, Margery and Doreen Fitzgerald attend classes but has made no mention of her own activities.

[324]

H. H. then enquires very civilly if the Ministry of Information keeps me very busy and I am obliged, in common honesty, to reply that it doesn't. Not, at all events, at present. H. H. says Ah, very non-committally, and adds that it's, in many ways, a very extraordinary war.

I agree that it is and we part, but not until I have recklessly suggested that he should come and meet one or two friends for a glass of sherry to-morrow, and he has accepted.

November 16th.—Ask Serena, across Canteen counter, whether she would like to come and help me entertain Humphrey Holloway over a glass of sherry to-morrow evening. She astonishingly replies that drink is the only thing—absolutely the *only* thing—at a time like this, and if I would like to bring him to her flat, where there's more room, she will ask one or two other people and we can provide the sherry between us. Then, I say—in rather stupefied accents—it will be a sherry-party.

Well, says Serena recklessly, why not? If we ask people by telephone at the last minute it won't be like a *real* sherry-party and anyway not many of them will come, because of the

black-out. Besides, one of her Refugees is perfectly wonderful with sandwiches, as she once
worked in a Legation, and it seems waste not to
make the most of this talent.

I suggest that this had better be Serena's
party, and that I should be invited as guest,
with Humphrey Holloway in attendance, but
Serena is firm: it must be a joint party and I am
to invite everybody I can think of and tell them
that she lives, fortunately, only one minute from
a bus-stop. She particularly wishes to have
Uncle A. and is certain—so am I—that the
black-out will not deter him for a moment.

We can get everything ready to-morrow,
when she will be off duty, says Serena—looking
wild—and I must take the evening off from the
Canteen.

Mrs. Peacock, who has been following the
conversation rather wistfully, backs this up—
and is instantly pressed by Serena to come too.

Mrs. Peacock would love it—she hasn't been
to a party for years and years—at least, not
since this war started, which *feels* to her like
years and years. Would it be possible for her
husband to come too? She doesn't like to tres-

pass on Serena's kindness but she and the husband practically never set eyes on one another nowadays, what with A.R.P.[1] and Red Cross and one thing and another, and she isn't *absolutely* certain of her leg now, and is glad of an arm—(very peculiar wording here, but meaning crystal-clear to an intelligent listener)—and finally, the husband has heard so much about Serena and myself that he is longing to meet us.

Cannot help feeling that much of this eloquence is recally superfluous as Serena at once exclaims in enchanted accents that she is only too delighted to think of *anybody* bringing *any* man, as parties are usually nothing but a pack of women. Point out to her later this not at all happily expressed and she agrees, but maintains that it's true.

Later in the evening Serena again approaches me and mutters that, if we count Uncle A. and J. L., she thinks we shall run to half a dozen men at the very least.

Tell her in return that I don't see why I shouldn't ask my Literary Agent, and that if she

[1] Air Raid Precautions.

doesn't mind the Weatherbys, Mr. W. will be another man.

Serena agrees to the Weatherbys with enthusiasm—although entirely, I feel, on the grounds of Agrippa's masculinity.

Remain on duty till 12.30, and have brief passage of arms with Red Cross nurse who complains that I have *not* given her two-pennyworth of marmalade. Explain that the amount of marmalade bestowed upon her in return for her twopence is decided by a higher authority than my own, then think this sounds ecclesiastical and slightly profane and add that I only mean the head cook, at which the Red Cross nurse looks astounded and simply reiterates that two-pennyworth of marmalade should reach to the *rim* of the jar, and not just below it. Can see by her expression that she means to contest the point from now until the Day of Judgment if necessary, and that I shall save much wear and tear by yielding at once. Do so, and feel that I am wholly lacking in strength of mind—but not the first time that this has been borne in on me, and cannot permit it to overshadow evening's activities.

[328]

Mock air-raid takes place at midnight, just as I am preparing to leave, and I decide to stay on and witness it, which I do, and am privileged to see Commandant racing up and down, smoking like a volcano, and directing all operations with great efficiency but, as usual, extreme high-handedness.

Stand at entrance to the underworld, with very heavy coat on over trousers and overall, and embark on abstract speculation as to women's fitness or otherwise for positions of authority and think how much better I myself should cope with it than the majority, combining common sense with civility, and have just got to rather impressive quotation—*Suaviter in modo fortiter in re*—when ambulance-man roars at me to Move out of the way or I shall get run over, and stretcher-bearing party at the same moment urges me to Keep that Gangway clear for Gawd's sake.

I go home shortly afterwards.

Gas-mask still missing, have only got temporary Registration Card, and find I have neglected to get new battery for electric torch.

Go to bed to the reflection that if Hitler

should select to-night for long-awaited major
attack on London by air, my chances of survival
are not good. Decide that in the circumstances I
shall feel justified in awaiting the end in com-
parative comfort of my bed.

November 17th.—Last night *not* selected by
Hitler.

Serena appears at what seems to me like dawn
and discusses proposed party for to-night with
enthusiasm. She is going home to get some sleep
and talk to Refugee sandwich-expert, and get
out the sherry. Will I collect flowers, cigarettes
and more sherry, and lend her all the ash-trays
I have?

Agree to everything and point out that we
must also expend some time in inviting guests,
which Serena admits she has forgotten. Shall
she, she asks madly, ring some of them up at
once?

No, eight o'clock in the morning not at all a
good time, and I propose to take her out for
some breakfast instead. Lyons' coffee much better than mine. (Serena agrees to this more
heartily than I think necessary.)

Proceed to Lyons and am a good deal struck

by extraordinary colour of Serena's face, reminding me of nothing so much as the sea at
Brighton. Implore her to spend the morning in
sleep and leave all preparations to me, and
once again suggest that she might employ her
time to more purpose than in sitting about in the
underworld, where she is wrecking her health
and at present doing nothing particularly useful.

Serena only says that the war has got to be
won *somehow*, by someone.

Can think of several answers but make none
of them, as Serena, for twopence, would have
hysterics in the Strand.

We separate after breakfast and I make a
great number of telephone calls, on behalf of
myself and Serena, inviting our friends and acquaintances to drink sherry—*not* a party—and
eat sandwiches—Refugee, ex-Legation, a gen-
ius with sandwiches—in Hampstead—flat one
minute's walk from bus-stop.

Humphrey Holloway accepts change of *lo-
cale* without a murmur, Rose declares that she
will be delighted to come—she has, ha-ha-ha,
nothing whatever to do and sees no prospect of
getting anything.

[331]

The Weatherbys also thank me, thank Serena, whom they don't yet know, and will turn up if Mr. W. can possibly leave his office in time. He hopes to be able to—believes that he will—but after all, anything may happen, at any moment, anywhere—and if it does, I shall of course understand that he will be Tied. Absolutely Tied.

Reply that I do, and refuse to dwell on foolish and flippant fancy of Agrippa, fastened up by stout cords, dealing with national emergency from his office desk.

Ring up Uncle A.'s flat, answered by Mrs. Mouse, and request her to take a message to Uncle A. which I give her in full, and beg her to ascertain reply whilst I hold on. Within about two seconds Uncle A. has arrived at the telephone in person and embarked on long and sprightly conversation in the course of which he assures me that nothing could give him greater pleasure than to accept my young friend's very civil invitation, and I am to present his compliments and assure her that he will not fail to put in an appearance. Frail attempt to give Uncle A. precise instructions as to how he is to find

the scene of the entertainment in the black-out
proves a failure, as he simply tells me that he
will be able to manage very well indeed between the public conveyance (bus from Kensington High Street?) and Shank's mare.

He further adds recommendation to me to be
very careful, as the streets nowadays are—no
doubt properly—uncommonly dark, and says
that he looks forward to meeting me and my
young friend. Affairs in Germany, in Uncle A.'s
opinion, are rapidly approaching a crisis and
that unhappy fellow is in what is vulgarly
known—(though surely only to Uncle A.?)—
as The Mulligatawny. Express my gratification
in words that I hope are suitable, and Uncle A.
rings off.

Later in the morning case arrives—which I
have great difficulty in opening, owing to absence of any tools except small hammer, and
have to ask if caretaker's husband will very
kindly Step Up—and proves to contain half-
dozen bottles of sherry with affectionately-
inscribed card from Uncle A.

Am deeply touched and ring up again, but
Mrs. M. replies that Uncle A. has gone out for

his walk and announced his intentions of lunching at the Club and playing Bridge afterwards.

Lady Blowfield, also invited, is grateful, but dejected as ever and feels quite unequal to Society at present. Assure her that this *isn't* Society, or anything in the least like it, but she remains unconvinced and only repeats that, what with one thing and another, neither she nor Archie can bear the thought of being anywhere but at home just now, waiting for whatever Fate may send. (Implication here that Fate is preparing something that will be unpleasant at best, and fatal at worst. Probably bombs.)

Assure Lady Blowfield untruthfully that I know exactly what she means, but am very sorry not to be seeing her and, naturally, Sir Archibald. *How* kind I am, returns Lady Blowfield— voice indicates that she is evidently nearly in tears—she can only hope that in happier times, if such are one day vouchsafed to this disordered world, we may achieve another meeting.

Tell her that I hope so too, and am rather shocked at hearing myself adopt most aggressively cheerful accents. Cannot suppose that these will really encourage Lady Blowfield to brighter frame of mind, but rather the contrary.

Final invitation is to Literary Agent, who much regrets that he is already engaged and would like to know how my new novel is getting on.

Well, it isn't very far on *yet*, I reply—as though another week would see it half-way to completion at least.

No? repeats Literary Agent, in tone if distressed surprise. Still, no doubt I realise that now—if ever—is the time when books are going to be *read*, and of course, whilst there are so few places of entertainment open, and people go out so little in the evenings, they will really be almost *forced* to take to books.

Am left wondering how many more people are going to dangle this encouraging reflection before me, and why they should suppose it to be a source of inspiration.

Review my wardrobe and can see nothing I should wish to wear for sherry-party. Decide that my Blue is less unbearable than my Black, but that both are out-of-date, unbecoming and in need of pressing, and that I shall wear no hat at all as none of mine are endurable and can never now afford to buy others. Ring at the bell interrupts very gloomy train of thought—Lady Blowfield outdone—and am startled at seeing familiar, but for an instant unrecognisable, figure at the door.

Turns out to be old school friend Cissie Crabbe, now presenting martial, and yet at the same time rather bulging, figure in khaki uniform.

Cissie assures me that she couldn't pass the door without looking in on me, but that she hasn't a moment to call her own, and that she expects to be sent Behind the Line any time now. Can only congratulate her, and say that I wish I was making myself equally useful. Suggestion from Cissie that I can sign on for four years or the duration, if I like, is allowed to pass unheeded.

Enquire what she has done with her cats, which are the only items I can ever remember in her life, and Cissie says that one Dear old Pussy passed away just after Munich—as though he *knew*—another one has been evacuated to the Isle of Wight, which Cissie feels to be far safer than Norwich for her—and the third one, a very, very individual temperament indeed and could never have survived for even a day if separated from Cissie—had to be Put to Sleep.

Consecrate a moment of reverent silence to this announcement, and then Cissie says that she can't possibly stop, but she felt she had to get a glimpse of me, she never forgets dear old days in the Fifth Form and do I remember reciting "The Assyrian Came Down like a Wolf on the Fold" and breaking down in the third verse?

No, I don't, but feel it would be unsympathetic to say so crudely, and merely reply that we've all *changed* a good deal since then, with which contribution to original contemporary thought we exchange farewells.

Watch Cissie walking at unnaturally smart pace towards the Strand and decide once and for all that women, especially when over forty, do not look their best in uniform.

Remainder of the morning goes in the purchase of cigarettes—very expensive—and flowers—so cheap that I ask for explanation and shopman informs me gloomily that nobody is buying them at all and he would be glad to *give* away carnations, roses and gardenias. He does not, however, offer to do so, and I content myself with chrysanthemums and anemones, for which I pay.

Pause in front of alluring window of small dress-shop has perfectly fatal result, as I am completely carried away by navy-blue siren-suit, with zip fastener—persuade myself that it is not only practical, warm and inexpensive—which it is—but indispensable as well, and go straight in and buy it for Serena's party.

Cannot regret this outburst when I put it on again before the glass in flat, and find the result becoming. Moreover, telephone call from Serena ensues later, for the express purpose of asking (*a*) How many men have I raked up? she's only got four, and five women not counting ourselves and the Refugees, and (*b*) What do I mean to Wear?

On hearing of siren-suit she shrieks and says she's got one *too*, and it was meant to surprise me, and we shall both look too marvellous.

Hope she may be right.

Do the best I can with my appearance, but am obliged to rely on final half-hour before Serena's mirror as I start early for Hampstead, heavily laden with flowers and cigarettes. Am half-way to Charing Cross before I remember Uncle A.'s case of sherry, when nothing is left for it but to take a taxi, go back and collect case, and start out all over again. Appearance by now much disordered but am delighted at having excellent excuse for taxi, and only regret that no such consideration will obtain on return journey.

Youngest and most elegant of Serena's Refugees opens the door to me—she is now disguised in charming pink check, frills and pleated apron, exactly like stage soubrette, and equally well made-up—we shake hands and she says Please! —takes all the packages from me, and when I thank her says Please! again—case of sherry is deposited by taxi-driver, to whom soubrette repeats Please, please! with very engaging smiles —and she then shows me into Serena's sitting-room, on the threshold of which we finally exchange Thank you and Please.

Serena is clad in claret-coloured siren-suit and delighted with herself—quite justifiably— and we compliment one another.

Strenuous half-hour follows, in the course of which Serena moves small bowl of anemones from window-sill to bookcase and back again not less than five several times.

Sherry is decanted—Serena has difficulties with corkscrew and begs soubrette to fetch her the scissors, but soubrette rightly declines, and takes corkscrew and all the bottles away, and presently returns two of them, uncorked, and says that her grandfather will open the others as required.

Is the oldest Refugee her grandfather, I enquire.

Serena—looks rather worried—says that they all seem to be related but she doesn't quite know how, anyway it's perfectly all *right*.

Accept this without hesitation and presently Serena's Refugees come in more or less *en bloc* and we all shake hands, Serena pours out sherry and we drink one another's healths, and glasses are then rushed away by the soubrette, washed and returned.

Serena puts on Six O'clock News—nothing sensational has transpired and we assure one another that, what with one thing and another, that Hitler régime is on the verge of a smash, but, says Serena in tones of preternatural wisdom, we must beware at all costs of wishful thinking. The German Reich *will* collapse, but not immediately, and anything may happen meanwhile. We have got to be prepared.

Assure her that I am prepared—except for loss of gas-mask, which has not yet been replaced—and that, so far as I know, the whole of the British Empire has been prepared for weeks and weeks, and hasn't had its morale in the least impaired by curious and unprecedented nature of Hitler's War of Nerves.

Serena, rather absentmindedly, says Rule, Britannia, moves small pink crystal ash-tray from one table to another, and studies the effect with her head on one side.

Diversion is occasioned by the soubrette, who comes in bearing succession of plates with sandwiches, tiny little sausages on sticks, and exotic and unfamiliar looking odds-and-ends at which Serena and I simultaneously shriek with excitement.

Very shortly afterwards Serena's guests begin to arrive—J. L. amongst the earliest, and my opinion of him goes up when I see him in earnest discussion with grandfather-presumptive Refugee. I think about the Nature of Eternity, to which both have evidently given a good deal of thought.

Mrs. Peacock comes, as expected, with Mr. Peacock, who is pale and wears pince-nez and is immediately introduced by Serena to pretty A.R.P.[1] worker, Muriel, with whom she thinks he may like to talk about air-raids. They at once begin to discuss Radio-stars Flotsam and Jetsam, and are evidently witty on the subject as both go into fits of laughter.

Party is now going with a swing and second glass of sherry causes me, as usual, to think myself really excellent conversationalist and my neighbours almost equally well worth hearing.

This agreeable frame of mind probably all to the good, as severe shock is inflicted by totally unexpected vision of old Mrs. Winter-Gammon, in rakish-looking toque and small fur cape over bottle-green wool.

Shall never believe that Serena really invited her.

She waves small claw at me from a distance and is presently to be seen perched on arm of

[1] Air Raid Precautions.

*Diversion is occasioned by the soubrette, who comes in
bearing succession of plates with sandwiches and
tiny little sausages on sticks.*

large chair—toes unable to touch the floor—in animated conversation with three men at once.

Am much annoyed and only slightly restored when Rose arrives, looking very distinguished as usual, and informs me—quite pale with astonishment—that she thinks she has got a very interesting job, with a reasonable salary attached, at Children's Clinic in the North of England. Congratulate her warmly and introduce Mr. Weatherby, whom I very nearly—but not quite —refer to as Tall Agrippa. Hope this *rapprochement* will prove a success as I hear them shortly afterwards talking about Queen Wilhelmina of Holland, and both sound full of approval.

Uncle A.—more like distinguished diplomat than ever—arrives early and stays late, and assures me that he has little or no difficulty in finding his way about in black-out. He takes optimistic view of international situation, says that it will take probably years to establish satisfactory peace terms but he has no doubt that eventually—say in ten or fifteen years' time— we shall see a very different Europe—free, he trusts and believes, from bloodshed and tyranny. Am glad to see that Uncle A. has every

[343]

intention of assisting personally at this world-wide regeneration and feel confident that his expectation of doing so will be realised.

He seems much taken with Serena, and they sit in a corner and embark on long tête-à-tête, while J. L. and I hand round Serena's refreshments. (J. L. inclined to be rather dejected, and when I refer to Plato—which I do solely with a view of encouraging him—he only says in reply that he has, of late, been reading Tolstoy. In the French translation, of course, he adds. Look him straight in the eye and answer, Of course; but he is evidently not taken in by this for one instant.)

Humphrey Holloway—original *raison d'être* for entire gathering—never turns up at all, but telephones to say that he is very sorry he can't manage it.

Am quite unable to feel particularly regretful about this—but find myself wishing several times that Robert could be here, or even Aunt Blanche.

Similar idea, to my great fury, has evidently come over Granny Bo-Peep, and she communicates it to me very shrilly above general noise, which has now reached riotous dimensions.

What a pity that dear, good man of mine isn't
here! she cries—she knows very well that I
should feel much happier if he were. She can
read it in my face. (At this I instinctively do
something with my face designed to make it look
quite different, and have no doubt that I succeed—but probably at cost of appearance, as
Mrs. W.-G. sympathetically enquires whether
I bit on a tooth.)

And poor dear Blanche! *What* a lot of good
it would do dear old Blanche to be taken out of
herself, and made to meet people. Mrs. W.-G.
doesn't want to say anything about herself—
(since when?)—but friends have told her over
and over again: Pussy—you *are* the party.
Where you are, with your wonderful vitality
and your ridiculous trick of making people
laugh, and that absurd way you have of getting
on with everybody—*there* is the party. How
well she remembers her great friend, the late
Bishop of London, saying those very words to
her—and she at once told him he mustn't talk
nonsense. She could say anything she liked to
the Bishop—anything. He always declared that
she was as good as a glass of champagne.

Think this Episcopal pronouncement quite

[345]

unsuitable, and have serious thoughts of saying so—but Mrs. W.-G. gives me no time.

She has heard, she says, that dear Blanche's eldest brother is here and wishes to meet him. Is that him over there, talking to Serena?

It is, and can plainly see that if I do not perform introduction instantly, Mrs. W.-G. will do it for herself.

Can only conform to her wishes, and she supplants Serena at Uncle A.'s side.

Serena makes long, hissing speech in an undertone of which I can only make out that she thinks the party is going well, and is her face purple, she *feels* as though it were, and whatever happens I'm not to go.

Had had no thought of going.

Everybody talks about the war, and general opinion is that it can't last long—Rose goes so far as to say Over by February, but J. L. tells her that the whole thing is going to be held up till the spring begins—at which I murmur to myself: Air-raid by air-raid the spring begins, and hope that nobody hears me—and then, says J. L., although short, it will be appalling. Hitler is a desperate man, and will launch a fearful

[346]

attack in every direction at once. His main objective will be London.

J. L. states this so authoritatively that general impression prevails that he has received his information direct from Berlin, and must know what he is talking about.

Mrs. Weatherby alone rallies very slightly and points out that an air-raid over London would be followed instantly by reprisals, and she doubts whether the morale of the German people would survive it. She believes them to be on the brink of revolution already, and the Czechs and the Austrians are actually *over* the brink.

She adds that she wouldn't break up the party for anything—none of us are to stir—but she must go.

She does go, and we all do stir, and party is broken up—but can quite feel that it has been a success.

Serena, the Refugees and I, see everybody off into depths of blackness unlit by single gleam of light anywhere at all, and Serena says they'll be lucky if they don't all end up with broken legs, and if they do, heaven knows where they'll go as no patients allowed in any of the Hospitals.

One of her Refugees informs her, surprisingly, that the black-out is nothing—nothing at all. Vienna has always been as dark as this, every night, for years—darker, if anything.

Serena and I and the Refugees finish such sandwiches as are left, she presses cigarettes on them and in return they carry away all the plates and glasses and insist that they will wash them and put them away—please—and Serena and I are not to do anything but rest ourselves —please, please.

Thank you, thank you.

Please.

November 21st.—Am startled as never before on receiving notification that my services as a writer are required, and may even take me abroad.

Am unable to judge whether activities will permit of my continuing a diary but prefer to suppose that they will be of too important a nature.

Ask myself whether war, as term has hitherto been understood, can be going to begin at last.

Reply, of sorts, supplied by Sir Auckland Geddes over the wireless.

Sir A. G. finds himself obliged to condemn the now general practice of running out into the street in order to view aircraft activities when engaged with the enemy overhead.

Can only hope that Hitler may come to hear of this remarkable reaction to his efforts, on the part of the British.